PORT MOODY PUBLIC LIBRARY

D0394474

THE GREEN CHILDREN OF WOOLPIT

ALSO BY J. ANDERSON COATS

R Is for Rebel

The Many Reflections of Miss Jane Deming

The Wicked and the Just

THE GREEN CHILDREN OF WOOLPIT

J. ANDERSON COATS

Atheneum Books for Young Readers
NEW YORK LONDON TORONTO SYDNEY NEW DELHI

atheneum

ATHENEUM BOOKS FOR YOUNG READERS † An imprint of Simon & Schuster Children's
Publishing Division † 1230 Avenue of the Americas, New York, New York 10020 † This
book is a work of fiction. Any references to historical events, real people, or real places are
used fictitiously. Other names, characters, places, and events are products of the author's
imagination, and any resemblance to actual events or places or persons, living or dead, is
entirely coincidental. † Text copyright © 2019 by J. Anderson Coats † Jacket illustration
copyright © 2019 by Victo Ngai † All rights reserved, including the right of reproduction in
whole or in part in any form. † ATHENEUM BOOKS FOR YOUNG READERS is a registered
trademark of Simon & Schuster, Inc. Atheneum logo is a trademark of Simon & Schuster,
Inc. † For information about special discounts for bulk purchases, please contact Simon &
Schuster Special Sales at 1-866-506-1949 or business@simonandschuster.com. † The Simon
& Schuster Speakers Bureau can bring authors to your live event. For more information
or to book an event, contact the Simon & Schuster Speakers Bureau at 1-866-248-3049 or
visit our website at www.simonspeakers.com. † The text for this book was set in ITC
Cheltenham Std. † Manufactured in the United States of America † 0819 FFG † First
Edition † 10 9 8 7 6 5 4 3 2 1 † Library of Congress Cataloging-in-Publication
Data † Names: Coats, J. Anderson (Jillian Anderson), author. † Title: The green children
of Woolpit / J. Anderson Coats. † Description: First edition. | New York : Atheneum Books
for Young Readers, [2019] | Summary: Twelve-year-old Agnes trusts a boy and girl with
green skin who claim they are fair folk, and that she is a fairy princess, but in their under-
ground world she finds great danger. † Identifiers: LCCN 2018061501| ISBN 9781534427907
(hardcover) | ISBN 9781534427921 (eBook) † Subjects: | CYAC: Fairies—Fiction. |
Magic—Fiction. | Identity—Fiction. | Fantasy. † Classification: LCC PZ7.1.C62 Gre 2019 |
DDC [Fic]—dc23 LC record available at https://lccn.loc.gov/2018061501

TO ROGER,
WHO WAS ALWAYS KIND TO ME,
AND TO MARSHA,
WHO WELCOMED ME
RIGHT FROM THE START

IN MEMORIAM

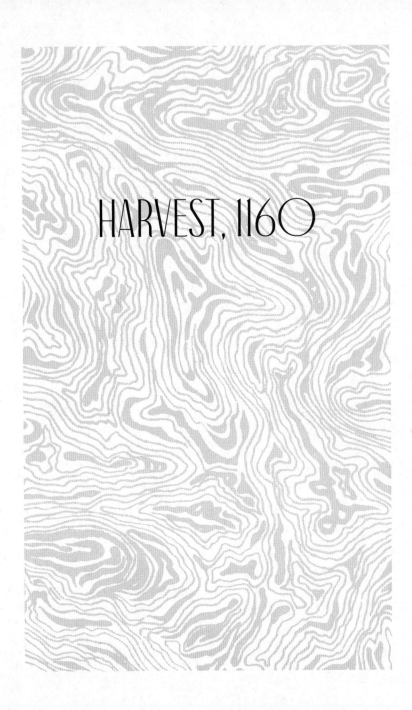

HARVEST, 1160

T oday's not the day to get lost in a story, Agnes Walter.
Everything feels like a story today, though.
It's hot in this wheat field, which makes me think
of deep, cool wells and the saints who look after
them, or a delicious patch of shade and the shadows
that play there, or the first snow of the year that brings
all the kids in Woolpit outside to make tracks everywhere so Those Good People can't tell whose house is
whose, at least for a while. There are a thousand stories
I could tell, but if you are a grown-up, *now* is never the
right time for such things.

My da is working ahead of me, swinging his scythe,
shush-shush, cutting close to the base of the stalks so
nothing is wasted. I follow him, stoop and gather, stoop
and gather, stoop—*ooooh*, look at those thin slivers of
wind chasing past like tiny threads of silver among the
husks of wheat.

I don't talk about how pretty the wind is anymore.

Not since Kate and Tabby started oinking at me and reminding anyone who'd listen that pigs are the only animals that can see the wind.

A cry rises somewhere distant. At first I'm sure it's a bird, but it keeps spinning up and falling like a baby's yowl but also like a dog that's gotten its tail caught in a door. Birds don't make that kind of sound, nor do beasts. Not even wolves. I trail to a halt and listen hard—not stooping, not gathering, not watching the wind—even though I've been warned twice already that there's to be no shirking. No foot-dragging. *Today's not the day to get lost in a story,* my da keeps saying, and the Woolpit mas have even less patience for stories than anything else, especially when my jammed-up words make everything I say sound like a falsehood.

I'll ask Glory. She's the best dog namer, straw braider, and butterfly chaser in Woolpit, and good at helping me stay in the here-and-now. She can't still be angry about what happened at the Maying. That was *months* ago, and I've begged her pardon and she gave it and surely she'll soon feel like making flower crowns again instead of always having a chore to do somewhere away from me.

I gather in a rush, leaving behind big swaths of cut wheat stalks, so I reach the top of the row when she does. I tug her sleeve and say, "Listen."

Glory jerks away. "What? What is it now?"

"You . . . you said you weren't angry anymore."

"I'm not. It's just . . ." Glory gestures at the long, narrow lines of cut stalks. "We've got all this work to do. And you missed a lot. Da won't like that."

Glory is gathering wheat behind her uncle instead of her da because her da is the reeve, and it's his job to see that the work gets done. He's the one hauled before Milord if it doesn't. She looks pink-cheeked and tidy like she always does. Not filthy and sweaty like me, even when I'm not in the wheat field. *A pretty girl turns heads,* she says, when she's never said that before this year. It's something those numbwits Kate and Tabby prattle, as if they have a single brain between them.

"Someone's crying. Far away. Don't you hear it?"

Glory muffles a groan. "I am *not* in the mood for one of your stories."

I study my feet. So she *is* still upset about what happened at the May Eve feast. Or mayhap she's thinking about her brother, even though we were both watching baby Hugh the day Those Good People breathed in his face and now he's in the churchyard under a sad little heap of dirt. There's only so many times you can tell someone you're sorry. Only so many times you can hear them say *that's all right* before you wonder what else you must do to make it so.

My eyes sting. Just because no one else can hear the crying doesn't mean it's not there. I'm the only one

I know who can see the wind curl past houses and fingers, through hair and leaves and fence posts. If it's not an animal making that sound, it must be a person, and the last person whose crying I ignored gasped his final breaths in shudders that grew ever slower, ever quieter.

By the time I tried to help baby Hugh, it was too late. Today someone is clearly in trouble, and considering how everyone else keeps working, how the reeve isn't blowing his horn all frantic and calling the name of someone missing from the field, I'm the only one who knows.

Crying twists up my insides now like it didn't before, but I can't just leave the harvest. Not when everyone helps. Not when there's no reason I can give that the reeve will see as a good one.

Only moments ago, so many things felt like a story, but not this kind of story. If something is not as it should be, Those Good People are likely near. It's one more reason not to say too much about seeing the wind. The Woolpit mas are very careful about keeping Those Good People at a polite, cautious distance. No one wants their cow to go dry or their granny to get a fever. If there's a shiny coin in a puddle or beautiful music just beyond the path, you'll do well to think twice before picking it up or peeking through the brush. It could be just what it seems—or it could be a trick meant to tempt you into promising something you don't want to part with.

Never call them by their name, Granny would say.

Speak respectfully of them always. With any fortune you will never meet one, but if you do, there will be no doubt what it is you see.

When the story is about a girl, you meet her doing ordinary things. Then the story part comes, and she must think carefully whether she should do the safe thing and keep feeding the pig, harvesting the wheat, and being an ordinary girl who stirs the beans sunwise just like her ma showed her so Those Good People can't sprinkle in thorns. Deciding isn't as simple as it might sound. The story part can lead to treasure as surely as it can lead to ruin, and at the very least she will get a scolding—and likely a smacking—if she leaves the wheat field when every soul in the village must help with the harvest.

The rest of Woolpit works on steadily. The reapers step and swing, step and swing, and wheat stalks fall around them like panes of sunlight. Girls and women rush armloads to older men who draw them into tight golden shocks and prop them up together. My dress is soaked with sweat. From today and yesterday. And the day before that. My hands are well bloodied, cuts atop cuts, from slips of chaff.

Most of the time the story's not about a girl at all. When it is, the girl has shiny yellow hair and clean feet and her da is the reeve. She is clever with her words and all the Woolpit mas fuss over her like a late-season peach. Everyone will notice her whether she does the safe thing or not.

But if the girl does the safe thing, there's no story.

At midday, I always go home and put the evening meal on the fire so it'll be ready when we stumble in late and exhausted. I'm supposed to go straight back to the wheat field and my stoop-and-gathering. All the way out to the house I hear the crying. All the time I'm getting the beans together and settling the pot on its little stand in the coals. The sound is faint but steady, gliding around corners and across fields like it's made of wind.

Glory told me to ignore baby Hugh. *He'll cry forever if you keep picking him up. Ma says to let him calm himself.*

We thought baby Hugh growing quieter was him going to sleep. That his gasping was the last of his cries.

It was, but not how we thought.

I cover the pot, pull the door closed, and follow the crying. I follow like Milord's dogs after a fox until the field is somewhere behind me and the heath opens out like a scratchy brown bedcover tossed gentle and wrinkly over a pallet. Beyond is the greenwood, dark and dangerous.

The crying drifts like a fog across the scrub-scattered plain. It's not just any voice. It's a *girl's* voice, and it's coming from the wolf pit.

The last time I was anywhere near the pit was two summers ago when Kate and Tabby dared me to get close enough to look in. Glory was there too, and she hissed and did urgent eyes at me because Kate and Tabby were *older* and they were *talking to us* and did I want to look like a *baby*?

The pit is a neither-nor, Granny would say. *Neither on the heath nor in the greenwood, and neither-nors are places you must watch yourself in. When something is neither one thing nor another, anything is possible.*

It was cold by the pit then, even for summer. Colder than it should have been such a short way into the greenwood, and as I edged near the long, jaggedy gap in the earth, there was a smell that hit me like a stone to the forehead. A damp, decaying smell, like old leaves pushed against a yard fence in November.

Like blood.

There were bones at the bottom. From wolves, of course, poor beasts who met their ends there, trapped where they could neither eat lambs nor cripple cows. But wolves did not have long, bleaching leg bones. They did not have skulls round and cracked like fruit.

That day two summers ago, I fled bawling and gibbering past Kate and Tabby as they pointed and laughed, as Glory stomped her foot with fed-up, helpless frustration. I flung myself away from all of them—toe-stubbing, lung-aching, skin-tingling—and I swore on every saint listening that I'd never go near the pit again.

Only someone else is crying today, and it's a girl.

It has to be, because there are words in those cries. There's a girl and the story will go like this: I'll rescue her and together we'll return to Woolpit and everyone will say how brave I was. How clever. My da will have to admit that sometimes it *is* a good day to get lost in a story because sometimes it's not quite the story you thought it was. Glory will stop rolling her eyes when I suggest a game we both loved only last summer and sighing long and loud when I say things like *we should make flower crowns for each of Mother's six piglets.*

The crying is loud now that I'm nearing the edge of the greenwood. It's not scared or sad, either. It's *raging.* That crying sends tiny chills down my back, and there's no question it's coming from the wolf pit.

Midday is a neither-nor. Neither morning nor evening.

The rotty smell is stronger here. It'll get in my hair. In the weave of my dress. It'll follow me home. Still, I creep to the edge. The pit falls away, down deep, twice the height of a man, and this edge has crumbled over time so it's rounded and impossible to climb.

There's a smudge of movement at the bottom. It's dark down there and I don't like the dark, but I peer in anyway. Just a little, in case I have to flee quickly.

Two faces appear. Small faces. Children. A boy, several summers younger than me. A girl about my size.

Their faces are green.

The girl gestures wildly with green hands and shouts

something that comes out raspy and hoarse. I scrabble away from the pit edge. Granny said I'd know in an instant if I met Those Good People. There would be no doubt.

It's all I can do to breathe. Anything that's not as it should be—strains of beautiful music, lights on the heath—that's when you must beware. *Stories keep you safe,* Granny would say, because following the music or the lights means Those Good People are luring you into the kingdom under the mountain, deep in the Otherworld. If you go, if you're tempted and not content with what you have, you'll end up their servant there. You'll be trapped forever, forced to work your fingers and feet to bloody stumps. You'll never see your ma and da again, or your house or your bed or your favorite doll made of straw that smells like wet dog.

You can weep and wail, and Those Good People will not care.

These kids cannot be Those Good People. Green is their color, but it's the color of their clothes, their jewels, their world. If they were green anywhere else, it would be in all the stories because it's the stories that keep girls like me safe.

But the stories would have girls like me stay *ordinary*.

I pull in long, long breaths until I can peek over the side once more. The green girl sees me and starts talking in a low, throaty growl. She's definitely saying words, but none of them make sense. The boy says nothing.

His face is in shadow like he's hiding from the light, but for half a moment I swear he grins at me, cold and cruel.

I hold out my hands, once peachy but now darkened by the sun. Cuts atop cuts. So many kinds of people travel the road past Woolpit to the abbey, especially at fair time. They're pale, freckly, rosy, and all shades of brown, but nary a one has been green. Not ever.

Those Good People love their trickery. Nothing gives them more delight than forcing someone to guess both their nature and their intentions.

Sometimes Those Good People reward mortal folk who do things they like, but they hate it when you come upon them unawares. Once you've offended them, you'd best give over whatever they demand as payment for the insult. Doesn't matter if you meant no harm.

Like me. Like now.

The safe thing is to leave them here. They're trying to lure me, somehow. Those Good People think of us like we think of mugs and tables and privy ditches. They grind through mortal servants like the millstone makes flour of the grain that Woolpit is even now cutting down. There is no escape once they have you.

Those Good People can make nothing of their own, Granny would say. *They need human hands to do their work. Even if they didn't, there's something they love about a servant. Someone to kneel and cringe. Someone who must always bow.*

But Those Good People would never blunder into a pit trap made to catch animals, and if for some reason they did, they'd find their own escape without asking the likes of me for help. These kids are thin and dirty. They might simply be children from a nearby village who wandered away from their own harvest. They'd never know the pit was here.

Although if they were from another village, I should be able to understand the girl. And there's no reason they'd be *green*.

I've never been anywhere but Woolpit, but I know there are other villages. I've known since my fifth summer when Kate and Tabby told me I was so ugly, it was no wonder my real parents didn't want me. That's when I learned that I was a foundling brought to my ma and da when I was so tiny I still had my birth-cord attached, and that's when I started crying because foundlings in stories were always sent away to make their fortunes or tormented by mas and das who didn't really want them, and even though getting lost in stories was good, at the end of the day I wanted a ma's lap to sit on and a da who'd show me how to plait fishing line.

But after my ma told off Kate and Tabby for being so hateful, she groaned down to her knees, took both my shoulders, looked me in the eye, and said, "You are our baby. Don't you listen to what *any* of those shrews say. You're ours and that's what matters."

The green girl starts whimpering, but softly this time. Like baby Hugh on that long, sweaty afternoon, writhing and gasping like a fish after crying himself raw. Glory and I had been so busy with our spinning that we didn't notice the iron poker had fallen off the cradle and Those Good People could get to him.

By then it was too late.

The green girl would not be so upset if she could get out of the pit any time she wanted. If the children *are* Those Good People and they're truly trapped down there, and if I free them, I can ask a favor and they will have to grant it.

The pit is too deep for me to reach in and help them up, and besides, I doubt I'm strong enough to pull out even the boy. If I'm going to get them free, I'll need help.

"Glory," I whisper, because she's the one who showed me how to grow big turnips and patch a dress so seamlessly you hardly saw the needlework. She's the one who'd ask me to play when the other girls' mas nudged them toward one another and away from me.

It's been months since the Maying and I didn't mean for it to happen like it did. The story was supposed to go like this: I'd tell the May King what Glory told me, that she thought he was comely and she'd like nothing better than to dance with him. He would hold out a gallant hand and they would leap and parade around the Maypole and the bonfire and he would declare his love for her but she would say she was too young to marry and he would wait for her and then in *many, many* years they would be married and I would make her so many flower crowns she'd need to give a few to me.

Instead the May King laughed hard and long right in her face and said something snide about cradle-robbing, which made Kate and Tabby double over laughing till they fell into each other like milk-drunk kittens. Glory turned red and ran home and refused to come back, even for the honey cake.

I can make it up to her now. I can bring Glory into this. If the green children do belong to Those Good People, and if she and I work together to save them from the pit, we can each ask a favor.

If they're not, if they're just hungry kids separated from their ma and da, kids who'll die here unless someone else happens along, Glory and I can help them out of the pit and bring them into the village. Everyone will stop the harvest to see us lead green children past. Their parents will weep and be grateful and mayhap offer something as reward. Woolpit will talk about me long after Christmas. Possibly even into next summer.

Mayhap forever.

There are precious few stories where girls help each other. They either fall out over a boy or there's some rubbish about one being prettier than the other, like that nonsense matters half a thumbnail. In fact, I can't think of

a single story—not one—with two girls who don't fight.

Not that there are many stories with girls in them at all.

This story will be different. It'll end with Glory and me friends again, just like it was. Just like it ought to be, the end.

When the girl's face appears over the pit edge, for the longest moment I don't think she's real. After everything I've gone through to get this far, for the one person who finally hears me to be a girl my age and not a drooling crone or a loathsome beardy beggar—it's a trick. It must be, and even now they're all down there laughing their guts out, wetting themselves at how big a fool I was to take any bargain the likes of them offered me.

Not just once, but twice.

I turn all rage to the—boy—beside me. Not a boy—a boy thing. But one look at him and right away I know he's angry she's here. It takes several heartbeats before I work out it's because he's angry that anyone is here.

No one was supposed to come at all.

The boy-thing sees me trembling and goes from rageful to spiteful in an eyeblink. His smirk is my brother's, too. Not just the curve of his jaw, his sturdy legs. His movements *and manners. There was a time I'd have given all the gold in the deepest hoard to see my brother's face again.*

But not this way. Never this way.

She's back at the pit edge now. Round cheeks and eyes like a pup on its hind end, waiting for a treat it'll never get.

A girl like me. Like I once was, down to the straw in her hair and the freckles on her nose. Like I can be again, if I think only on her blood.

Precious few things gain and hold attention in the Otherworld. One is a bargain. The other is a sacrifice.

I spot Glory coming out of her uncle's house and hurry up the rutted road, panting like a winded horse. "Glory! Hey!"

She takes several more strides toward the wheat field before she slows, and slows, and finally whirls on her heel. "You're following me again. We talked about this. How sometimes I want to be by myself."

We didn't talk. Not exactly. Glory told me and I nodded because I felt tiny and buzzing and she was batting me away, and if I buzzed louder, she'd squash me.

"I found out who was crying. It's—"

"Da won't like knowing you're here," Glory cuts in. "You're supposed to be at the harvest."

"Aren't you supposed to be there too?" It's a real question, not a mean singsong not-a-question like Kate and Tabby ask, but Glory scowls.

"*I've* come to start supper. *You* are shirking. Chasing crying that isn't there so people will ask you about it."

A year ago I could have told what I saw. All of it. She'd have believed me. Now I must prove it to her, and I must be careful how I do it. A year ago I wouldn't have even had this thought, that I must keep things from Glory till she has a chance to see for herself. It makes my stomach hurt.

"It's children," I reply. "A girl and a boy. I think they're lost. They're stuck in the wolf pit. Will you help me get them out?"

Glory softens. "Children?"

"Yes!" I grip my apron so I don't grab her sleeve. "Your da has that rope, doesn't he? We can lower it down for them."

"This isn't a story, right? We'll get to the wolf pit and there really will be kids trapped there?" Glory glances around like someone's watching. "Because I swear to all the saints, Agnes, if you're making this up . . ."

But I'm already hurrying. I'd know the way to Glory's house blindfolded, and I skip and grin so big my face hurts. Glory is speaking to me again. We're off to do something together, like we haven't in so many months that even my ma noticed and I had to pretend everything was fine.

Once Glory fetches the rope, we set off toward the woodland path that'll take us the long way to the wolf pit, far from the wheat fields. She insists on carrying the heavy coils herself, so I'm out ahead. A little smug. Her eyes will go huge when she sees they're not just kids. Glory will squeal and hug me for bringing her into this story, even if I did it with a small bit of trickery.

The brush shifts and I skid to a stop. The reeve is blocking the path. Arms folded. Shaking his head in a slow, disappointed way. Glory and I all but shared a cradle and I've had my share of scoldings from her da, but his eyes glide over me and rest on her.

"What's the meaning of this?" he asks.

Neither of us replies. I'm trying to come back from the part of the story where the girls were hugging and being cheered by the whole village, but it's jumbled with the part where they're deciding what favor to ask of Those Good People, and this is usually where a grown-up will shout something like *speak up!* or *answer me!* They don't see I'm trying. Often they don't care.

It's quiet too long, because the reeve sighs and peels the rope from Glory's shoulder and says, "Shirking the harvest. I expected better of you."

Glory's eyes fill with angry, stubborn tears. Something hard as a nut is growing in my throat. She'll never forgive me if she's scolded for that, of all things.

"I heard them crying." I haven't planned these words the way I plan most of what I say, but there's no time. "In the wolf pit. Children. *Green* children. A boy and a girl. We needed the rope to pull them out. I was going to put it back."

Glory rounds on me. Her face is going red in splotches. "You promised it wasn't a story. You *promised.*"

The reeve sighs deeper. He drops the rope in Glory's arms and curtly tells her to hang it where she found it before taking herself directly to the wheat field. Then he grabs my elbow and guides me firmly away, leaving Glory on the path, narrow-eyed and furious.

She was going to forgive me and I could say *the end* and we could start whole new stories together, just like before.

There's not enough room on the path for the reeve and me to walk side by side, so I'm stumbling in the verge, lashed by branches. I have to make this right. I tap his shoulder and start babbling, "I, ah, well, Glory, she—"

"Hush." The reeve doesn't say it mean. He is not that kind of grown-up. But he says it sharp and simple and final, and I do as I'm told. I know what's going to happen now. As baby Hugh lay still and cold in his cradle, the reeve warned me what would happen if I spoke false about anything at all, big or small, ever again.

Now I'll have to wear the mask.

The mask is the size of a water bucket. It's made from strips of metal bent into a cage that's fastened to some-one's head with three sturdy leather straps. On the front there's a huge metal tongue, lolling like a dog's, painted red, and there are bells hanging off the cage, dozens of them, so wherever you go, people will know to turn and look.

The reeve has no pity for me as he tightens each strap. "You should have thought about this before telling tales again."

The story is spilling out of me now. I'm telling him everything as he pulls me by the elbow from the shade of his house toward the wheat field. "You have to believe me. No one else heard them crying. They'll die if no one helps them climb out."

The reeve won't look at me. He leads me jangling back to the field.

The worst part of the mask isn't that it's made for grown-ups so it bangs and scrapes my forehead and its sharp edges dig into my shoulders. It's not even that everyone will hear me long before they see me and know exactly what happened, or that the straps are pulling my hair, or that I'll have to pour water through the bars for a drink and it'll itch down my neck and make me damp for the whole fortnight I must wear it.

The worst part is walking behind the reeve, him not bothering to slow because he knows I must follow, whatever his pace, walking toward my ma and da who right now are happy because they have no idea what a mess I've made of things.

Like with baby Hugh.

The reeve wept, but mostly he seemed resigned. That little grave won't be the only one they visit in the churchyard. He nodded, red-eyed, while I told both him and Glory's ma about the bee, how Hugh was fine until it disappeared into his cradle and then he started screaming and swelled up so bad he couldn't even pull in a breath, all while Glory and I looked on in horror. But that's when Glory's ma swiped at her tears and started blustering about how bees were not to blame, how Glory and I let the iron fireplace poker fall off the cradle and Those Good People must have blown their cold breath on poor Hugh.

Salt and iron would have kept them out! she thundered. *Did you two never listen to your grannies?*

I walked behind the reeve that day to my house. Through the door I could see Ma spinning and Da whittling aimlessly. *You are our baby,* they always say, and in those moments before we got inside I whispered it to myself because one day I might do something so terrible that they might not think so anymore, and then I'll be no one's baby.

*S*omeone's coming. Finally. I'd started wondering if that girl was smarter than she looked and with one glance at us—at me—fled back to her hearth or her spinning or her playing and pretended she was never here.

Like she knew, somehow, what I'd come for. What I meant to do to her.

But there's a crashing in the greenwood above, men shouting at one another to beware the edge of the pit. A dog whines, harsh and high like it's being dragged closer, unwilling. Dogs don't like places like this.

People should pay more attention to dogs.

Besides the girl, the only soul that has so much as cast a shadow above me was a pig. It was a she-pig, a sow, and she studied me over the pit edge, grunting low. If that sow were a person, she'd be warning me away.

Soon the girl will peer over the side of this pit once more. A part of me wants to be sorry for her. If that is something I can still want, perhaps there's hope for me yet. She has done nothing to deserve what will happen to her.

Neither did I. Nor did any of us.

The boy-thing grins from his place against the pit wall. I can barely look at him. There's only one reason he's wearing my dead brother's face. My brother did not take their bargain, and the fair folk mean to remind me what befell him every time I look upon this boy-thing.

All of me hardens and I start yelling. I beg for help. I beg for mercy. I scream for my ma and da, lost so long. The boy-thing giggles. He understands what I'm saying, but the men above us won't. They will only hear my voice. They will hear the rawness of it. The fear. It comes from some deep well inside me. Some terrible, scabbed-over place, half healed and aching.

They will hear my voice and they will find us. The girl, and the men of this place I have finally, finally come back to. They will see only two children, lost and alone. They won't know one has come for something unspeakable and the other is not a child at all.

They won't realize any of it till it's too late.

While I was gone putting on supper and being caught red-handed and blundering badly enough to make Glory even more angry with me, Da kept cutting wheat. All afternoon I tried to catch up gathering, but there are so many cut stalks that I'll be here all night finishing my work. No one will help me. *You should have thought of this natter natter natter.*

The sun has been going ever so slowly down, and when it's dark the reeve will blow his horn and everyone else can stop work for the day. The Woolpit mas are already busy whispering. There's but one grown-up who would have helped me, and that was Granny. Days like this are when I miss her most of all. The Woolpit mas would always make the safe choice and stay home to do the milking. They would rather have a good wheel of cheese than a story to tell.

The same was not true of Granny.

I catch a whiff of that leaf-rot smell just as someone

hurries past me, bumping my arm so I fumble my stalks. Across the field, men are lowering their scythes and women have put aside their gathering. There's an excited burst of chatter and soon everyone is rushing toward the edge of the field where Glory is standing with her da—and the green girl and boy.

The children each wear too-big cloaks that are clearly borrowed, and both have pulled the heavy hoods over their faces as if it's January. They clutch the wool with green hands, turning away from the gathering villagers who hover while trying to seem polite and not suspicious. Even though that damp, rotty stink hangs on those kids like they climbed out of the grave and not the wolf pit, soon I can't see them for the crowd.

Now there'll be questions. When there are foundlings, there are always questions, and the Woolpit mas are not known for asking with anything like gentleness.

Nothing harmed by courtesy, Granny would say. *Doesn't cost a penny to be kind. Especially when you don't know what you're dealing with.*

The reeve breaks away from Glory and makes his way toward me. He winces, then gestures for me to turn. When I do, he unbuckles the leather straps and gingerly lifts the mask off my head.

"Off home with you now," he says. "Your day's work is done."

The sun is going down, but there'll be plenty of light

left to work for some time. This is an apology and I should accept it. Thank him. But it's hard to stay standing. Purple spots all spinny in my eyes. Wearing the mask for even half a day is easily the worst thing that's ever happened. I'll do anything to keep from having to wear it again.

I totter a few steps toward Glory. This is how the story will go: She will see me and feel terrible. She didn't believe me on the path. She turned her back on me. But something small made her wonder. So she went to the wolf pit anyway, and when she saw that the green children were real and in need of help and none of it was a tale, she felt a wave of sorrow as she helped them climb out. *I've been treating Agnes so badly these last months*, Glory would have thought. Now we'll hug, right in front of everyone, especially those nose-in-the-air Woolpit mas who always want to believe the worst of foundling me.

It's neither day nor night as the sun bleeds out over the horizon. It's both. It's neither. Same as how I found the green children, but in a way I didn't find them. It's both and neither unless Glory says something now.

But what Glory's telling the crowd is how she alone heard the children crying in the greenwood. How she found them lost and afraid, how they wept until she brought them something to shield their eyes from the light. No one else thought to help them. Only she had the wit.

I back away. My legs barely hold me up. The crowd goes blurry. Glory doesn't notice me. Last summer she would have noticed. She would have shoved through the villagers and pulled me by the hand till I was next to her. She'd have shushed everyone and made them stay quiet till I worked out what I had to say.

But Glory is the girl in this story now. She rescued the green children. She can ask of them a favor and they will grant it, if they are Those Good People, or she will be feasted and cheered by their ordinary mortal parents once they are found and reunited. Her da is the reeve, and he will see to it.

Just once I want to be the girl in the story. Just once I want someone to hear me and *believe*.

The reeve said I could go home. So I go. Now I'm under the bedclothes. It's quiet and dark. No one gawking at me. It's stifling and damp and I can hardly draw breath, but after today, after the mask, I just might have to stay here till winter. Mayhap longer.

My pallet crunches with the kind of heavy, narrow footfalls that can only come from hooves. I claw the bedcover off my head and nearly bump snouts with Mother. Pigs in Woolpit are allowed to wander where they please. I must have left the door open, which Ma will give me an earful about if she learns of it, but I'm glad Mother is here. She's such a good listener that she doesn't care how I think things at her instead of say them with words that catch and trip over one another. She is always ready to get lost in a story. Last month, Glory said she was too old to talk to pigs, but I'll never be too old to talk to Mother.

Mother shuffles toward the shelf that my da built against the far wall that holds our spare pot and some earthenware bowls. Her wide bottom bumps the wall and a handful of things tumble down. I mutter a swear and rush over to see what broke, but all that fell was a ratty basket for berrying and a pair of iron knitting needles that Granny gave me when I was small. She often watched me and Glory while our mas were busy, and we were a handful and she needed us to be still, so she taught us to knit.

I'm about to put the needles away since knitting is a winter task, but Mother makes a rusty sort of squeal at me, low in her throat, and I hold them crosswise the way Granny would always keep a pair tacked to her door.

Salt and iron will ward Those Good People away, Granny would say, *as long as you owe them nothing. They have no power unless you give it to them. If you've wronged them, if they have a claim on you, they cannot be stopped till they have what's due them.*

But Granny also said things like *Do them a good turn and you will prosper. Your cow will always give fresh milk and your seams will be straight and strong.*

I wrap my needles in a scrap of wool and push them far back on the shelf. Close enough to ward away any of Those Good People with mischief on their minds, but far enough to be the show of goodwill I intend.

The green children may not have forgotten I was the one who really found them. They may want to pay me a visit. I even know what favor I'd ask.

Please have Glory be the kind of friend she used to be.

They don't come and they don't come. At length the Woolpit mas start up their whispering as all of us stoop and gather in the wheat field. *They were squinting and stumbling, poor lambs. Like the light hurts their eyes. No one can get a sensible word out of either child and they won't eat a crumb. Milord has taken them in. Doesn't do to make enemies, does it?*

The green children are at the manor house. They might as well be on the moon.

It's almost midday and my arms are full of scratchy wheat stalks when the reeve taps my elbow and says, "Come with me."

My neck is still raw from the mask. My ears still ringing. But my ma and da don't need another visit from the reeve, so I give my stalks to the binders and follow him.

"Hurry," he says, but then he must notice how I'm dragging my feet because he adds, "No one's angry at you. Your lord has asked for your help."

Something inside me glows pink and warm at the idea that a man like Milord needs my help. I'm expected to do what I'm told. Hardly anyone asks for my help.

Most of the time there is never a good reason for one of us from Woolpit to be called to the manor house. Either you've done wrong and you must account for it at Milord's court, or it's quarter day and time to pay your taxes. Or sometimes if a pig moves into your shed and the Woolpit mas decide you must have stolen it.

The story goes like this: Just days after I arrived, a sow turned up in our yard. Her ear wasn't clipped and she had no marks or brands. My da asked everyone he knew, but the pig belonged to no one in Woolpit, or at the abbey, or anywhere nearby. Still the mas whispered, muttering because my ma had taken in baby me when who knows what the raggedy woman who brought me had been and done. My da had to go to the manor house and swear before everyone that he had not taken the pig unlawfully and would give her up to her rightful owner within a year and a day if that person came forward. No one claimed her, though, and when I could talk I started calling her Mother, and she has never left.

Today is not quarter day and I'm too young to owe taxes. I've done nothing wrong that I haven't already paid for. If I'm being brought to the manor house, it's because of the green children, and that is a *very* good reason.

I follow the reeve through the weathered wooden gate. There's a faint whiff of that rotty smell as we cross the muddy yard, and it gets stronger as we step through a big oaken door that groans on rusty hinges.

I've been to the manor house yard many times, but never inside. I want to marvel at every last thing, but the reeve pulls me into a hall and toward a trestle table that's piled with more food than I've ever seen in one place. Crouching under the table, poised to flee like stable cats brought indoors, are the green girl and boy. Each is gripping one of the sawhorse legs like someone recently tried to drag them out by force.

The reeve guides me by the elbow to the head of the table. "Here she is, my lord. For all the good it'll do."

Just the mention of him and I go still. There are so many places Milord has to be, so many manors to visit, that he never stays too long at any one of them, especially in places like Woolpit. But he's here now, striding into the firelight in a fine woolen tunic and taking up so much space that I kneel well before he gets anywhere near me.

"Rise, child." Milord chuckles, and when I do as I'm told, trying not to think how I'll be eating beans for supper while he sits down to a spread like this, he gestures to the green children beneath the table like all of this is ordinary somehow. "Will you greet them and ask if they'll come out? This food is for them. It's been days since they've had a proper meal. I'm at a loss as to how to get them to stop hiding and take even a bite of bread. As I understand it, you being here will do the trick. Since you were the first one they saw."

I go cold all over. The green girl saw me at the top of the pit. Then I went away. *I* know this part of the story—the reeve, the mask, the Woolpit mas penning me in so I couldn't lift a wheat stalk without them knowing—but *she* doesn't. The girl never put eyes on me again, and I know what Glory must have said. What she's *been* saying. The green children likely believed her. They'd have no reason not to.

If the green children want me here, they mean to punish me for abandoning them.

"They cried when the other girl walked through the door," Milord says mildly. "The reeve's child. The pretty one who said she found them."

Milord must not have a granny. Otherwise he'd know that Those Good People would never eat any food but their own. If they ate mortal food, they would not be allowed back under the mountain, just like mortals who ate food offered by Those Good People would spend eternity in their underground court.

I can't say any of this, though. So I just shake my head.

"You're *refusing*?" Milord asks, but he sounds more bewildered than angry, like someone saying him nay is unthinkable.

My belly turns over. This is a neither-nor. I can offend neither the green children nor Milord without consequences. I must do *something*, so I kneel and peer under the table while I plan what I'll say. The girl turns toward me like I'm a sister or cousin she hasn't seen for seasons. The boy shifts so his face stays in shadow.

Carefully I tell them, "Milord would like to welcome you to his table. No need to be frightened."

Right away the girl crawls forward. The boy is on her heels. Once they're out, the rotty, damp smell is overwhelming, but for the longest moment all I can do is stare.

It wasn't a trick of the light. They are *green*.

There's no calling them pale or gray from some illness. Their skin is the color of leaves uncurling in spring, shiny almost, though their hair is a rich mossy color. The girl's is long and loose, wavy like it's been braided of late, and the boy's tumbles to his collar like he belongs here at the manor. Not cropped like my da's or any of the village men. Their clothing is an endless wash of greens, all different, woven in a shimmery pattern that ripples like the scales on a fish whenever they move, and well made in a way that makes me think of hawking and feasting, not hacking at wheat in a field.

Neither Milord nor the reeve seems to notice the smell. I must fight to keep from covering my nose with my cloak as the boy slides onto one of the benches and gives the girl a long, steady look. The girl grabs my wrist and guides me to the opposite bench. I nearly pull away from the shock of it, but her touch is no different from Glory's, or my ma's. The green of her is no different from the pink of me. She sits me down so we're together there, side by side.

For months now I've been alone with my spinning and alone in my playing. Without Glory to insist I be included, there's always a reason I'm not allowed to come along or join the chore or play the game. I cannot help but smile sidelong at the green girl.

A look crosses her face. Like she's a cat and I'm a small scurrying sound in a hay pile. Then I blink, and she's studying her hands folded in her lap.

"Well, they came out," the reeve says to Milord. "As I said, for all the good it'll do you."

The boy looks to be eight or nine summers. He's small and thin, like a bird, like a boy whose ma doesn't want him playing out of her sight.

Milord puts a gentle hand on my shoulder. "Eat something. Show them there's nothing to be afraid of."

I don't need to be asked twice. There are two pewter plates on the table, and I pull one toward me and fill it with handfuls of bread and half a roast capon and a scoop of that savory whatever-it-is that smells like spices I can't even guess at. Once there's no more room on the plate, I carefully place it between the green girl and me. I mean to wait, to give her the first choice, but

I can't help myself and grab one of the capon legs. I've never had a whole leg for my own, and when I bite into it, the meat melts in a slurry of tender skin and butter.

It would be something to be the daughter of a house like this.

The green boy catches my eye, then goes back to looking at the food like it's rubbish from the midden piled up before him. It's almost like he heard me think it, then made it loud enough to push down other thoughts, and I know I shouldn't think anything of the sort because wanting things is how Those Good People snare you.

Fine gowns and servants to make the porridge. There'd be a lot less porridge, too, and a lot more meat. People would listen when I talked. They wouldn't dare not, or I'd be interesting just because I lived here, and they'd want to listen.

He's smiling. For the smallest instant. Isn't he? I take a big bite and chew it slow, tasting salt and spice and warmth and safety. The leaf-rot smell tickles my nose and all I can think is how much I want to live somewhere like here forever.

The green girl uses the handle of her meat knife to push the heaping pewter plate so it's entirely in front of me.

Milord lifts his brows at the reeve, but the reeve muffles a groan like he's fighting for patience. "No offense intended, my lord, but this is by no means proof.

They've been told by their parents to be wary of strangers. Take it from a father who lost a son. It's little wonder to me they'll touch nothing."

"There's no further proof I need," Milord replies airily. "They can't take the light. They won't eat our food."

I stop chewing. If the green children are Those Good People and they've come to punish me, they'd have done it by now. So mayhap they want me here because they know the truth, that I'm the one who found them, and Glory is the liar this time.

Mayhap they think to reward me after all.

The green boy cocks his head of a sudden, sniffing like I would if there was a spiced cake nearby. He gets up and comes around the table toward the girl and me, and while I'm struck by the green of his eyes, he pulls from my apron two fistfuls of ripe bean pods still on their stalks from when I hurriedly wrenched them out of the garden this morning.

My mouth is full. My hands, too, so I can't stop him. I can't tell him that those beans are for my family's supper, that I was supposed to add them to the porridge at midday and I forgot and my ma will give me an earful.

The green boy jams his fingers into the stalks, trying to pry them open as if the beans are in there instead of the pods. Even the reeve is staring openmouthed. There are other villages, surely. But other villages where kids don't know that beans come in pods instead of stems is a story no one would believe.

At length the boy slumps on the flagstones, defeated, and lets shredded stalks fall through his hands. He slices a tiny smile at the girl, and I am about to gasp but the rotty smell rises and the smile never happened because it's a plea, begging her to help, begging *someone* to help.

The green girl hisses and swipes a pod from his hand. She slits it with a thumbnail and wolfs down the beans raw, without butter or salt or any kind of sauce. While she finishes the beans I brought, Milord speaks quietly with a servant, and in a short while, the servant brings a basket heaping with bean pods. The girl eats those too without a glance at the capon and pie on the table, or a look at the boy. He does not reach for the basket. He barely moves at all.

"I'll hold a feast," Milord murmurs. "Not here, of course. Somewhere grand. Men will come from all over. The king may even show."

"You'll set about finding their parents, you mean," the reeve says.

"Their parents? Whyever would I do that?"

The reeve's face goes ruddy. "Do you mean to tell me you're not even going to *try* to find their parents? Begging your pardon, my lord, but I will speak against it because that is not right."

"Tom." Milord chuckles. "I will not find them."

"These kids are not . . . what you think they are. They are just children. It's not like we've never seen little ones in this state. During the old king's reign, when things were bad, don't you remember seeing them along the roadsides? In ditches? A few were even this sort of color. Paler than this, but green." The reeve's voice warps. "Likely from eating nothing but grass when there was no one to care for them."

I put down my bread. I've heard those stories. I don't like them.

"Tom—"

"Look anyway," the reeve says through his teeth, but then he must remember who he's talking to because he gets redder and adds, "That is, the only right thing is to look anyway. You don't want it said you're stealing children. Do you?"

Milord sighs. "Very well. But when I *don't* find their parents, I won't hear any more said about it. In the meantime, my steward will find them a place to lodge in the servants' quarters."

"What of Agnes?" The reeve tips his chin at me, and the green girl looks up from searching the empty pods for more beans.

"Walter's daughter? Oh, she can be gone once she's eaten her fill. She's been most helpful, but I imagine she'll be of more use in the wheat field now that I have the answers I wanted."

I'm wondering how much bread I can sneak into my apron, when the green girl shoves a hand into mine and grips hard. Her eyes get hard too, and she pulls me down to the floor and starts wailing like someone twice bereaved.

The flagstones are cold beneath my knees. I think to put an arm around her, but I'm not sure she'd welcome it.

Those Good People do not cry.

The boy's face is utterly still, like a carving from church. He's not sad or scared. It's like he feels nothing at all. The girl is holding my hand so tightly it stings, and part of me is happy because Glory and I once had a game where we'd see how long we could go holding hands before we had to break apart. But I shiver a little because Glory and I were all but sisters and I just *met* this girl.

"In case you hadn't noticed, the children are very attached to Walter's daughter," Milord says to the reeve, sly and smug. "Perhaps she could stay here in the servants' quarters with them."

If I stay here, no one in the village will know this story, that Milord needed my help, that I got to eat my fill at this table, that the green children wanted me instead of Glory. *That girl and her stories,* the Woolpit mas will say, but it will be the absolute truth. The reeve will have to swear to it. In front of everyone. Including Glory.

Glory will surely want to make flower crowns with

the girl who got to fill her guts with honey cake at the manor house instead of endlessly talking about nothing with Kate and Tabby.

Milord brought the green children here and nothing ill has befallen him. He did not tack iron needles to his door or bury salt at his threshold. The girl is holding my hand like we're friends already. If she's one of Those Good People, I dare not offend her. If she's not, she will have an easier time as a foundling if there's someone nearby who understands.

"Ah . . ." I raise my voice so I can be heard over the green girl's crying. "The children could come to my house. My ma and da could look after them while you find their parents."

Milord frowns. "You should not promise for another, child. Besides, I could not ask it of them. Not with winter coming on. These two will be better off here."

The green girl bawls louder and her grip tightens.

"They took *me*." My heart is racing. "Not just for winter, either. Forever."

The reeve gives me a rare smile. "Agnes has a point, my lord. There's no one better suited to care for found-lings *while you look for their parents* than the two gener-ous souls who took in the last one."

That story goes like this: A bruised, hollow-eyed woman turned up on the heath dressed in scraps of a worn dress and gibbering like someone who'd seen war.

She had a days-old infant strapped to her chest and went from house to house begging someone to raise it. Some of the Woolpit mas felt sorry for her. Most muttered mean things that even now make my ears go hot. No one opened their door for her—until my ma. My ma not only held out her arms for baby me, but invited the woman in to warm her feet and have some ale and talk about it. But as soon as she'd handed me over, the woman backed away, shaking her head. The Woolpit mas thought to question her, but neither she nor her body was ever found.

"Very well, Tom." Milord smiles faintly. "If you want to look the fool, so be it. Bring a cart around and take them to Walter's place. I won't search forever, though. They'll be back here by spring."

The reeve nods, bows, and moves toward the door. Milord follows, and as soon as the grown-ups are gone, the green girl stops crying. She doesn't whimper and tremble and at last get control of herself. She *stops*, like a candle flame snuffed out, and abruptly lets go of my hand.

The green boy is still sitting amid the shredded bean pods. He picks one up and digs in his thumbnail so juice runs down his hand. I try to think of something Granny may have said about beans, but all that comes to mind is *pity the wolves, yes, but it is their sacrifice that saves us.*

I am close now. It won't be too much longer.

At first I thought this Agnes was more clever than she looked, disappearing from the pit and sending a sacrifice in her place. Especially as the golden-headed fluffwit pranced and preened along the edge, telling her daddy to lower the rope a certain way, to pull the boy-thing up first because he was littler and therefore more afraid. As if she knew his heart somehow.

That girl wouldn't do. She wouldn't do because she was not the one who heard me calling, and she would not take a hint.

That's when I worked out there was no cleverness in the fluffwit turning up at the pit edge. It was all fortune, and I cannot trust fortune. Not with this boy-thing beside me. Not given what he wants.

It took three days to get Agnes here. The lord of this place is like a garden worked through with manure; any fertile seed will grow. I had to be careful, though. Directing

the boy-thing's glamour is risky, and if I'm caught, he'll turn the full weight of its power on me. I had to nudge the idea to fetch Agnes into the chieftain's head in snips and pieces, and I paid for it well when the boy-thing put on that show with the bean stalks. No mortal child would look for beans in stalks instead of pods. He may as well have announced himself then and there.

If he was permitted to speak above the mountain, doubtless he already would have.

After all this time, such a piddling while as three days should not bother me. But I am no longer in the Otherworld, where time moves however the fair folk mold it. I have till All Hallow's Eve. If I haven't done what I've come to do, I'll be worse than lost.

Now Agnes is at the table, loading her apron with bread and meat. Her hands are warm, rubbed well with sheep grease, and her hair is the color of a tiny nameless bird. It's hard to believe I was ever like her. That I could smile at a stranger and invite her into my home.

I was, though. But I was also the kind of girl who could wring a chicken's neck and crush mice that I found in the grain stores.

The kind of girl who does what she must to survive.

P ast the mill, up the path, and there's my house. My ma and da step outside as the cart rolls by the shed and into the yard. They must have come directly from the wheat field since their faces are so red and sweaty. The reeve leaps down and pulls them into the doorway, muttering something about *poorly nourished* and *in deep distress* and *a little mothering*, how my ma of all the mas in Woolpit is best suited to caring for them *given their circumstances*.

"You'll not be able to understand anything they say," the reeve tells my ma as the three of us climb down from the cart. "They can make themselves understood with gestures, though, so you'll need patience."

Mother the pig lumbers around the corner of the house and stops at my side like a dog might. The green girl studies her for so long that I have a sudden, wild thought that perhaps she has never seen a pig before.

Mother makes a low, screechy sound, then nips me on the meat of my lower leg.

I choke on a squeal and clap a hand over the wound. Mother . . . *bit* me? The green girl hisses something in that strange tongue, and Mother turns and hurries toward her byre.

"Their parents are likely from one of the Flemish settlements nearby," the reeve goes on. "Or it's possible they strayed away from travelers or merchants on the road to the abbey. Sir Richard has already sent a rider asking after lost children. I cannot imagine they'll be long at your hearth."

"We're happy to keep them for Milord," says Da. "We'll treat them like our own."

It's easily the most words together I've heard my da say in some time, but they're words that warm me like a drink of steaming cider. Perhaps he said something like it when he got home from plowing and saw baby me in Ma's arms. My da says nothing he doesn't mean, and when he says things like that, I know he *is* my da no matter what. Other than little children whose mas haven't had time to have more babies, I'm the only kid in Woolpit without at least one brother or sister. But I should have one. When I came along, my parents had a baby of their own, Martin, only a few months old. He took sick and died not long after I arrived.

I wish I'd known him, or that other babies had been

born, but Glory has always been like my sister. Now, at least for a little while, I have a brother *and* a sister. If the green children are just kids and Milord doesn't find their parents, or if they're dead, mayhap they could be my brother and sister forever. If everyone is talking about the green children and they're living at my house, whether they're ordinary kids or Those Good People, soon enough the whole village will be talking about me as well.

Glory will never be able to stay away then.

The reeve climbs back onto the cart and takes his leave. While I cautiously pull up my skirt enough to get a look at where Mother nipped me—*nipped* me!—my ma beckons to the green girl like she cannot smell the leaf-rot stench, and the girl edges toward her like a stray cat to a flake of fish.

"Come in, that's right." My ma holds the door open. "Sit by the fire. You and your brother too. What can we call you, child?"

Never give them your name, Granny would say, *or they will be able to demand of you anything. Never ask them theirs, or they will punish your rudeness.*

But as I'm about to remind my ma that the green children cannot speak how we do, the girl slips her hand between my ma's sturdy, gnarled fingers and says, "Agnes."

My mouth falls open, but the green girl presses

close to my ma and looks up at her like a newborn lamb. A softness is falling over my ma, thick and drapey like a blanket, beginning with her stern mouth and following itself upward, to her well-creased forehead. The pig bite on my leg throbs and I smell the leaf-rot clear and sharp, stingy in my nose hairs.

"No." I can't help it. There are four Elizabeths, three Katherines, and a startling seven Matildas in Woolpit, but I'm the only Agnes.

My ma puts her arm around the green girl's shoulders and gives me a ma look. "No? *No?* This poor child is lost, far away from her parents, and you cannot even welcome her into our home with a little courtesy?"

"Beg pardon," I whisper, "but I'm the only Agnes in Woolpit."

"Well, not anymore you're not." My ma perches the green girl on the hearth bench as I wince at the smell. The boy is still standing in the doorway. Like he's waiting for something.

Or being *kept outside* by something.

My da guides the green boy in by both shoulders and sits him on the bench next to the girl. He's creaky from having to stoop along cutting wheat all day, and his face shows it, but that rotty smell surges and he grins like a month of mutton suppers. "What about you, son? What can we call you?"

The boy's gaze flicks to the shelf at the far end of

the room where my knitting needles are. He makes no reply.

"Emmmmmmmm . . ." The green girl is trying to say something, but it's like she's got a mouthful of fresh honey and the sounds are all gummed up in it. Like me when I try to speak without planning my words. The green boy's fingers flash—did he *pinch* her?—and the girl flinches and presses her lips shut.

"Martin, then." Da claps him on the shoulder, his voice wavering the smallest bit. There's a quiet look between my ma and da. They're remembering the baby who slipped away so small and who also had that name. The big brother I should have had.

"Agnes." My ma tries to blink back her teary glisten. "Please fetch our guests some bread."

I stand up. So does the green girl.

My ma chuckles and says to her, "No, child, Fair Agnes will get the bread. You are the guest."

I'm wringing my hands in my apron. It's not the green girl's fault that her name is Agnes, too. It's a silly thing to care about when the green girl is like me. A foundling. Only she's old enough to be scared, and I was so small I never knew different. "They'll just eat beans. Raw beans. And I don't want to be Fair Agnes. I just want to be Agnes."

"Well, we have to tell you apart from our guest some-how," my ma replies firmly. "You'll be Fair Agnes for your hair, and she'll be Green Agnes for her . . . herself."

The girl grins like this is the first thing that's happened all day worth smiling over, and I feel barely a handswidth tall. If I were lost, far from Woolpit, far from my ma and da, far from anyone who could even understand me, and there was a girl being snippy about her *name* of all things—well, I wouldn't like her very much. I wouldn't be too happy to be her foster sister. Or her friend.

If I were one of Those Good People, I'd be sure any reward due her would be the kind that ends up a punishment.

So I put on a big smile and turn to the girl. "Please forgive me. That wasn't nice. I'll go pick some beans for you and your brother."

"Good. You do that." My ma waves me toward the door. She's still fussing over the green boy and girl and doesn't look up when I fetch the ratty basket from the shelf.

The girl does, though. Right as I'm leaving, she darts a look at me from under my ma's arm. It's triumphant, like she won a footrace at midsummer or just got made May Queen, and all at once I shiver like someone walked over my grave.

fter all this time, I knew certain things would be different. *This house is colder than our last one, and a strange shape. There's no earthwork or palisade wall, but there's a fire to tend and a pig fattening on* the hoof and pots and spoons. *There is light here, honest-to-goodness* sunlight, *and I could cry for how the prickle of the last of summer on my skin is like a nice, long embrace from an old friend you never thought you'd see again.*

There is the food I cannot eat. Bread I recognize, and meat, and it is real *bread and meat and not just leaves made to seem grand by the fair folk's glamour. I want to eat it. My hands tremble and my mouth waters, but one bite of it and I'll die on the spot.*

There will be conditions, *the king said.* Otherwise you'll try to cheat the bargain.

Best of all, there is her. There is the big woman with the red face and misshapen nose, smelling not of damp

and rot but sweat and meat and wool. She is nothing like my first ma, but she is a ma. You can see it in the lines of her face, how she's always staying up worrying over big things she can't control and small things she tries to. You can see it in the dirt beneath her nails. The way she rarely sits down.

Beside me on the bench, the boy-thing perches like a watchful cat. Already he's using his glamour to put ideas in these people's heads. He made this da give him the name of his own dead son. He did it with a smile. I have till All Hallow's Eve, but I must not take that long. The boy-thing is dangerous. Even in this boy-shape that hides so well what he really is.

While we were in the pit, the boy-thing kept whispering. No one's coming, *he said*. They're all gone. Long dead. Keep calling for them, though. Nothing is more amusing than someone who thinks there's hope. *If he'd have just stood there, I'd have given up. Instead I kept screaming so I couldn't hear his voice. Someone would hear me. Someone would come. I just never thought it would be a girl with a ma like this ma. This is a ma who loves her child. You can see it in how she keeps watch on the door. How she wants her daughter to share and show courtesy. This is a ma who will miss her child and grieve her when she's gone.*

Unless this ma never knows that her old daughter is creeping through the half-lit corridors of the kingdom

under the mountain, living in fear of the walls, working her fingers bloody and raw.

This ma will have a new daughter. One who never left. One who's always been here. That new daughter's forever under the mountain will finally come to an end. The old daughter's will be just beginning.

I blink awake. The room is lit up enough that it must be daybreak. The harvest. I'm late. That's going to mean a thrashing. Two thrashings: one from my da and another from the reeve. I fling back what little I have of the bedcover, then sit up slowly and try to make sense of what I'm seeing.

My ma and da are still asleep in their bed, two dark hills of blanket that the light seems to avoid on purpose. Martin's eyes are closed as well, but the green girl is standing by the hearth bench. The fire is banked, glowing softly, and the space around the door is black. It's nowhere near dawn, but the house is lit faint and steady. It's a half-light, like early morning, but there are no cheerful oranges or pinks in it. A neither-nor if ever there was one. The light is hard enough that I must squint despite how dim it is—and it's *green*.

A scream creeps up my throat and comes out a strangled, wrenching squeal.

"Shh." The green girl puts a finger to her lips and beckons me closer. Her hood is up, and she carves a stark figure in the dim against the strange glow.

I'm not sure whether the safe thing to do is refuse or obey. So I shh. I move closer. My heart is skidding because this has to mean that the green children really are Those Good People and I can ask of them the favor they owe for helping them out of the pit. *Please have Glory be the kind of friend she used to be.* Those Good People may be devious and petty, but if they owe you, they will pay in full.

When I get to the bench, the girl drops to her knees like I'm Milord.

"Oh, your grace, I'm so glad I finally found you," she says in a fierce, happy whisper, perfect and clear like she's Glory, like she's *me*, and while I stand there with my mouth open, she rises in a graceful rustle of cloth. She is nowhere near the quivering, weeping girl who fell to pieces on the manor house floor, or the big-eyed child too nervous to get near my house. "Your parents will be beside themselves to know you're well and to have you back with them."

"My parents are over there." I flummox a gesture at the bed. "Asleep. How can you—the reeve said you couldn't—"

"I had nothing to say to them," the green girl cuts in. "Only to you. Breathe in deep."

I do it, even though the room smells like garden muck when you turn it in the spring.

"Good. Now you'll understand everything I have to say. Keep your voice down, though. No one else must overhear." Her eyes go quick to Martin asleep near the fire, and she pulls in a long breath like she's preparing to lift something heavy.

"Wh-what's happening?"

"Don't be frightened." The girl steps closer. "We've come to return you to your real parents before anything ill befalls you. So please listen."

"But who are you? Why are you *green*?"

"You ought to know better than to ask someone like me who she *is*."

I go cold. Fight to breathe. "It's just . . . you were in the pit. Those like you would never get trapped in the pit."

"We wouldn't," the green girl says with a wisp of a smile, "unless there's a reason to do it. Unless someone must find the daughter of the king and queen under the mountain and bring her home."

I peer at her, bewildered, till her coy look falls to utter frustration. "You, simpleton! That's you! Those people asleep in that bed? They're not your real parents. You're not their child. You're really the princess of the court under the mountain."

For a moment it stings—*you're not their child*—and it takes up the whole world, even if it's true. I love my ma and da, but I was someone else's baby before I was theirs. I could belong to the woman who came raving to Woolpit. Or she could have found me under a black-berry hedge. Or she could have stolen me out of a cot-tage. No one is sure, not even my ma.

Which means I'm *no one's* baby. Kate and Tabby say it all the time in that cruel way they have, too singsongy, too wide-eyed-smiley for it to be kind.

Glory said it meant I could be *anyone's* baby. This was after she overheard Kate and Tabby taunting me one more time, and she told them to go fall in the stream. She said it in that fierce, protective way that made me start crying all over again, but relieved, like Glory's mere saying of it took away the truth of Kate and Tabby's saying completely.

Something small and hopeful turns over deep within me. Glory was once the kind of friend who would face down older girls. I could be anyone's baby. Including the king and queen under the mountain.

A foundling's a bit of a neither-nor as well.

I have so many questions. None of them are safe. Those Good People set traps for mortals for all sorts of reasons, from need to want to just plain fun, and the green girl is like Glory, fast and nimble with words.

They will twist the truth, Granny would say. *They will dodge and duck and withhold, but they will never, ever lie.*

Finally I say, careful and polite, "I don't understand."

"Your nursemaid lost track of you when you were very small. No one could find you. The king and queen had given up hope of ever seeing you again." The green girl's eyes are wide and earnest. "You were not born to the people you call your parents. You were found somewhere and brought to them. That's true, isn't it?"

The story has never gone any one way. Always it depends on the teller. So I say, "No one's sure where I come from, exactly."

"Hmm." The green girl nods knowingly. "I bet your ma says it doesn't matter. It does, though. Down deep, you want to know who you really are."

Be wary when Those Good People flatter you, Granny would say, but the idea of knowing who I really am makes me feel half a dozen things at once, and none of them are flattering. I've imagined my first parents a thousand different ways, but never in a way where I might have to choose.

The green girl is waiting. Big eyes, folded hands. Hopeful. This could be a trick. It could also be a test. There could be a reward as sure as there could be a punishment. Those Good People do not lie, but the king and queen under the mountain would not be careless enough to lose track of a child. They would have ridden out long ago to recover me and—hopefully—reward my ma and da who took care of me in the meantime.

Granny would say . . . Oh saints, what *would* Granny say?

"Please," the green girl whispers. "They miss you so much."

There's a surge in the leaf-rot smell, a wave of it that hits me like a drench of stale water, and all at once I see myself in a long white dress made of something thin and silky, not dirty—*never* dirty—hands smooth and uncut, dancing, dancing, a trestle piled with food fifty times as grand as Milord's at the manor house. Laughing, glorious, the center of the room, everyone saying my name, everyone asking what I think.

I hold out a hand. Only I don't. My hand reaches out on its own. Toward the green girl's. Closer. She grins harsh and triumphant and—

My leg stings where Mother nipped me, and I bend down to rub it and I'm back in myself. In the hard, dim green light.

The girl's eyes are closed. All she's been doing is standing there, but she's breathing hard like an ox in a yoke. Martin stirs in his sleep and she goes so still that even I hold my breath. As he quiets, she regards him like she would happily murder him where he lies. The look is gone in an instant, and her smile is helpless now. Wry, and a little pained.

"They were wrong, I suppose," the green girl says in a small, sad voice. "I was sent to fetch you because your parents thought you were more likely to trust a girl like you. They were sure you'd never follow a strange man away from the only home you'd ever known." She shrugs, downcast. "But you don't trust me."

"That's not true!" I step toward the green girl. "Why did the king and queen not come themselves?"

"They cannot."

The leaf-rot smell tickles my throat. Glory didn't believe me when I told her about the green children. Believing someone when it's hard is no simple matter. Only *not* believing someone just because it's hard makes me no better than a Woolpit ma.

I lick my lips. "Can I think about it?"

"It's already been longer than is good for us," the green girl says. "Your brother and I were days in the pit even before you ran away and left us to our fate."

"He's *your* brother. Isn't he? He's green like you, after all."

The girl makes a sound, something between a cough and a laugh and a snort. She shakes her head, slow and solemn.

A brother. I should have a brother. His name should be Martin, and he should have twelve summers, just like me. If you believe the Woolpit mas, the raggedy gibbering woman who left me behind returned in the blackest part of night and gave him the evil eye, to wither him so I might grow strong.

"We were *days* in the pit," the girl repeats, sharper this time, "and then days in the manor house before you could be bothered to turn up."

"Bothered?" I flinch. "No, it wasn't like that! It—"

"And now you don't even believe me." The green girl turns away. "You don't think any of this is true."

I plan carefully what I want to say, even though I'm quiet for too long. "It's a lot to consider, is all. But I know you . . . your kind, they do not lie."

The girl's lips twitch, like she's trying not to smile. "That's right. They don't. They *hate* lies."

"How do you know it's me? I'm different from when I was a baby."

"You heard me calling from the pit, didn't you?" the green girl asks. "When no one else in all of this place did? Nobody else heard me because no one else *could*."

The rotty smell hangs like a fog. Glory thought the crying was a tale. Believing was hard, so she decided not to. I scratch at my leg, where it stings a little. Last summer, Glory would have believed. Even if she hadn't heard the crying herself. She'd have taken my word for it and we would be here together.

"Think on it. Just do it quickly. We'll take sick from the salt and iron if we stay away from the mountain too long." The green girl nods at Martin on the pallet. "He'll get the worst of it. This is his first time out. He hasn't built up defenses. There's a chance he could die."

"Then why did his ma and da let him come with you?"

"He begged them. He wanted to play the hero. Besides, they were sure you'd come right away." She sighs. "I promised to keep him safe."

Martin looks so small curled there. I can't be the one to cause him any suffering. He's here because of me, whether I'm his sister or not. "I'll think on it. I promise. But if I stay, will you grant me the favor that you owe? For saving you and Martin from the pit?"

"Only you didn't save us, did you? The reeve's daughter is the one who brought the harvesters. She brought the rope. It's she who gets the favor, if there's a favor to be granted."

Glory's favor will have something to do with being pretty. If I want her to be the kind of friend she used to be, I'll have to make it up to her some other way. All on my own.

"You going to tell them?" The green girl gestures to the big bed.

I touch the fiery line of raw skin across my collar. My ma and da will not hesitate to fetch the reeve if I repeat any of this. They cannot be seen to coddle me. Not after baby Hugh.

They're not your real parents.

"No," I tell her.

"Good. Best to say nothing till you've decided whether to go away under the mountain or stay here."

The girl smiles shyly. "I hope you decide to go home, though. All of us will be so much happier."

As the green glow fades, I curl up tight on the bench for a long time in the cool darkness, thinking on what she said, like I promised. I may tell stories, but I'm no liar. The pig bite on my leg aches in dull waves as if it's trying to get me to think of nothing but Mother, but I pay it no mind. I could be anyone's baby, and Those Good People do not lie.

I just might be the lost princess of the kingdom under the mountain.

T he haze of dawn promises a blister of a day. My head aches from directing the boy-thing's glamour, but at least he didn't wake up and catch me at it. If he knew I was trying to convince Agnes to believe, to nudge her with something that isn't mine to use, he would do things to make this ma and da ask questions no one could answer. He would cause them to turn us out.

He might do it anyway. That would be most pleasing to those like him who find struggle amusing, and he is here for no other reason.

Agnes kneels by the fire to eat her porridge, but before she can begin, this ma bids her to go pick beans for us. Beans touch neither sun nor earth and grow in their own kingdom hidden from the light. They keep me bound while they keep me alive.

Before long, Agnes brings the beans in her apron. The boy-thing lifts an eyebrow, and this ma is glamoured enough that she portions them out unevenly. Agnes pauses *in front of us with two unequal shares. She will see them as the same, and she will give the bigger one to him. She lingers over the idea of a brother and he knows this. He won't even eat what she gives him, but he does not want me to have enough.*

I say nothing. If she even suspects, all is lost.

But Agnes blinks, touches the back of her leg, then shakes beans from one palm to the other till the shares are even. She motions for each of us to hold out cupped hands.

The boy-thing's eyes narrow.

"Do you have enough to eat, Green Agnes?" this ma asks, and the gentleness of it, the kindness, sets my roots in deeper.

I hold up my hands and smile and nod. She pets my hair and bustles away, calling for this da who is in the yard trying to find the pig.

That pig has no liking for me, though I've done it no ill.

Agnes crouches by the fire, eating her porridge with her fingers. "If he is my brother, and if I am one of your kind, surely I can know his name. Yours as well. Your real names."

My mouth falls open. It's like she shoved an apple there.

"I know why you gave my parents false names," Agnes goes on, and there's a smugness in her voice, like she's patting herself on the back. "You don't want them to be able to ask a favor. But I can know. Can I not?"

No. No. Everything is in motion. The first thing of hers is already mine. I have taken Agnes from her. But none of it will matter if she does not believe. All she has to do to ruin everything is shrug and ignore me. All she must do is let All Hallow's Eve come and go.

I've been quiet too long. My mouth open and flapping. Already a veil is falling over her, and she is making a decision about me. About the story I'm telling her.

"Senna." It's out before I can call it back. Before I can reclaim it and keep it where I can protect it. The last of me, before I made that foolish, foolish bargain.

Agnes licks the porridge off her fingers. Every time I decide she is the gods' greatest fool, she does something that makes me wonder just how clever she is. She turns to the boy-thing and asks, "What about you?"

He buzzes a series of swears that make me cringe, but he says them with a smile, one Agnes cannot help but return because she has no idea that she's just been insulted.

"He hasn't learned your tongue," I tell her. "Don't worry, though. Once you're under the mountain, you'll be able to understand each other just fine."

"But you and I have no trouble—"

"It's best if you keep calling him Martin," I cut in. "He likes the name. He says it makes him feel more like your brother. You lost one brother named Martin. Now you have another."

It works like I mean it to and Agnes drifts away on it, her face going vacant like a cloudless sky. I have survived under the mountain by listening especially well when voices are lowered. I've secured this chance to leave because I'm willing to do what's necessary, never mind the cost.

The boy-thing makes a cackle-cough sound, but all his glamour can do is make things seem like something else. He cannot change one thing into another, he cannot speak, and he cannot simply snatch me back into the Otherworld. Not until All Hallow's Eve. Not unless I fail.

There are conditions, after all.

"Senna." Agnes repeats my name, and in a blink it's like this house isn't here, nor this village. None of these things that have been built by those who came after us. It's a meadow again like I remember, and Acatica is calling to me and we are running and laughing with all the day ahead of us. "It's a strange name. But I like it. It makes me think of trees on a blowy day. What sort of name is it?"

"An old name." Dust now. Like everything that once lived here. "A very old one."

"Are you my sister?" Agnes asks hopefully. "Like Martin is my brother?"

"More . . . a friend of the family. Someone who'd like nothing better than to help you make your way under the mountain."

"You should tell Ma you can talk," Agnes says, as this ma is coming back in with a bucket of water. "Ma, guess what? The green girl can talk!"

This ma gives her a stern look. "No stories, Agnes Walter."

Agnes turns to me, waiting, but I slit open another pod with my thumbnail and pry out the beans.

"Go ahead. Show Ma." Agnes says it gentle and encouraging.

"Enough." This ma is different from my last ma, but a ma voice is a ma voice.

"But she can*!" Agnes flings her hands around like she's trying to say something, but it must be caught in midair. "Like we can. With words. Words we know!"*

"Stop it!" This ma is tossing wilted greens into the bucket she just emptied. "Don't you think that if she could talk, she'd tell us who and where her parents are?"

I smile outright because I already know where my parents are. They are right here, preparing to harvest wheat. This ma is speaking of my old parents, though. The lord of this place will never find them. He would have to dig for a thousand years.

"If she could speak, she'd have done so when Glory Miller first found her in the wolf pit." This ma shoves the bucket of scraps at Agnes. "Mother hasn't come along this morning. Go put that out for her, and I'd best not hear any more of this rubbish again."

Agnes starts to say something. It comes out all in a hash and she presses both hands against her face. Then she hangs her head and shuffles out the door. I curse myself. I should have jumped up the moment I saw this ma with the bucket. Agnes loves that pig dearly. But no hurry. Soon enough that chore will be mine as well. So will the pig, and it won't be a pet much longer.

There's a dull chime from outside as Agnes comes back in. She turns to me while securing her hood. "That's the horn. We have to go. Are you ready?"

"Don't be foolish," says this da from the doorway. "Green Agnes and Martin will be staying here today. They've been through a lot. They need their rest."

"What?" Agnes's round face is turning red. "But it's the harvest *and* no one—"

This da grabs her by the arm and marches her outside. She stops shouting as soon as they leave because he is talking now, reminding her that we are guests and she won't have any harsh words for us. This ma puts a hand on my cheek. Her skin is rough but I'm melting beneath it, sniffling, because it's been a thousand years and more since someone has touched me with anything like kindness.

"Oh, sweeting, don't cry." This ma wipes my tears with her sleeve and that makes me weep all the more. "Stay close to the house, all right? Don't lift a finger. If you need anything, Fair Agnes will be along at midday to see to the evening meal."

I nod. This ma hovers her arms around me for a hug, not sure what I'll do if she pulls me close. I can't help it. I fling myself up and into her arms and I have her, I have a ma again, and I might never let her go.

Over her shoulder, I catch sight of the boy-thing on the bench. He lifts a single eyebrow, taunting, but I don't open my arms until that dratted horn sounds again and she's gone, trundling in her too-big leather shoes, promising she'll try to convince the reeve to let her come home early to check on us.

The moment we're alone, the boy-thing is off the bench and into the yard. He has no liking for being indoors, but he's also toying with me. With glamour, he can make anything seem like anything else. He can put ideas into people's heads with just enough of a whisper that it's like the thought was their very own.

I can do none of those things, and he will win the bargain.

All Hallow's Eve will come and I will not have done what I must do. He will wring every drop of misery he can out of me and Agnes both, and then he will snatch me away, back to the kingdom of the fair folk under the mountain. There will be no exchange and I will look upon the rats with envy.

I peek out the front door. The boy-thing is far off down the yard, poking around the shed where this da was looking for the pig earlier today. Then I go to the shelf at the back of the house and pull down a parcel. Two needles, poorly forged but iron nonetheless.

There are conditions, but one of them is not that I must play fair.

The story is going like this: Those Good People do not lie. Senna said I was the lost princess under the mountain. I was brought to my parents as a foundling, and it's never sat right with the Woolpit mas. There's no reason it's not true, and several reasons it is. *The end* must be that I truly am the lost princess under the mountain.

It seems like forever before it's midday and the reeve blows his horn. The grown-ups head for their bread and ale and I set off for home to put on the supper. I still don't see why Senna can't put the pot of beans on the fire, since she's not being made to help with the harvest or do anything, really. I asked Ma, but all I got was a slap across the mouth and a warning not to be discourteous to our guests.

A princess under the mountain would never do chores.

There's a smear of green in the doorway of my house.

Senna is sitting on the step, her head in her hands, shiny hair spilling across her shoulders.

"This is worse than I thought," she whispers, and it's hoarse and helpless and she says it to the ground just like I did, trying to get the words out to Glory's ma about baby Hugh. I wriggle past her into the house and bite back a shriek.

Martin is folded in a pale, twitching lump on my pallet by the fire. The leaf-rot smell is weak, like a dead mouse in your neighbor's wall, but it still stings the back of my throat.

"What happened?" I sink down and shake him gently, but he's barely breathing and his eyes don't open and he's icy to the touch—*oh saints, like baby Hugh.*

"He's in a bad way." Senna follows me in and stands beside me.

"But you said he'd only get a little sicker the longer he was here!"

"That's how it's supposed to be." She runs a hand through her hair. "I don't know what's wrong."

"Is it that smell making him sick?" I ask.

"No!" Senna whirls to face me. "You—ah—what smell?"

I sit back on my heels, gnawing my fist. Baby Hugh was fine until he wasn't. I should have noticed the iron poker had fallen off the cradle, only I was trying to get Glory to play a guessing game and she was giving one-word answers because it was right after the Maying and she had given me her pardon for what I did, only she hadn't, not really, and it was all I could think about. How if Glory wasn't my friend anymore, I'd have no one.

Martin clutches his middle, moaning softly. Not moaning. *Buzzing.* He makes a weak grasp at Senna, his fingers like claws.

"I could get him some chamomile." I flutter my hands over him uselessly. "My ma sometimes brews it in hot water when her insides are hurting."

"Nothing's going to help but going home," Senna replies. "Will you take him?"

"Now?"

"Yes, now!" Senna snaps. "You're really going to make him suffer like this? Your own brother? Who risked his health to come save you?"

Martin is dying before my eyes and I'm not sure how exactly *I'm* in need of saving but none of those questions will come together right.

"I can't manage him alone. Not in this state. He's too heavy. We'll have to carry him together." Senna gives me a searing look. "Don't worry. The king and queen would never keep you with them if you're unwilling. It's not as if they've been hoping against hope you were somehow still alive all these years and not long dead from the salt and iron. They'll deny you nothing, even if what you want will break their hearts."

Keep a respectful distance, Granny would say. *If they want you near, they mean you harm.*

But Granny also said Those Good People do not lie. It must be true that I can bring Martin to safety and the king and queen will let me go if I choose. It must be true that Martin will get sicker if he's kept above the mountain.

It must be true that the king and queen want nothing more than for me to come home. *You are our baby,* they will whisper, and they will mean every word, even when I ask a simple question that deserves a reply and not a slap to the face. They will hold me so close I will never worry whose baby I am ever again.

"Right. Right." I swallow hard. "I'll help you. Let's hurry."

"He's too sick to walk. We'll have to carry him in the blanket."

There's a whisper of that rotty smell, and a story tries to happen—funeral procession open grave mothers crying all mothers everywhere—but the pig bite throbs once, deep and wrenching, and the story-bits fall away, more confusing than anything.

"Are you coming?" Senna's voice is raw.

I grab one end of Martin's blanket and heft him up. Crumbs of dirt fall from the underside of the wool. The ground beneath him is all torn up. There's dirt under his nails, too, but I dare not hesitate over my brother one moment longer. He's the same pale green as the beans I keep picking for him, shiny and waxen, and already it might be too late to save him.

He won't be like baby Hugh. Not if I can help it.

Senna and I hurry along paths and through fields toward the heath. I'm not even sure Those Good People can die, but one look at Martin and I don't want to find out the hard way. I couldn't face the king and queen under the mountain knowing their son—my brother— was dead because of me.

The wolf pit is just as I remember. Cold and dark and deep, not a stone's throw into the greenwood. Every hair on my arms is standing up. That dank smell hangs like a soaking blanket.

There are bones, Granny would say, *because there is sacrifice. Pity the wolves if you will, but they do not pity you.*

Senna leads me stumbling to the edge of the pit and lowers her end of the blanket-sling so I must do the same. Martin lies folded on the ground. He's still buzzing faintly, eyes in slits, and he doesn't seem in his right mind. I hang back. My skin is crawling.

"This is where we cross," Senna says, and after a long moment I work out all the meanings in those few words.

"Isn't there a hill?" I ask. "Granny always said . . . your people, *our* people . . . they live inside a mountain. That's where the kingdom is. Hidden away in the Otherworld. Deep underground."

"There *was* a hill. Then there was a war." Senna gestures at the pit standing dark and open, waiting, like a newly dug grave. "Now there is this."

I edge a step back. Toward the safe thing. Toward Woolpit and my hearth and Glory's massive sighs and the endless hand-slicing work in the wheat field.

But it's not the safe thing. Not anymore. I'm one of Those Good People now, and I promised to help my brother get home so he can recover. Going back on a promise is the worst thing I can do.

No. The worst thing I can do is ignore someone who's crying. Someone who might be *dying*.

"We'll need to lower him gently," Senna says. "Let's get him on his feet."

Martin is buzzing, low and stuttery. Somehow, in spite of what happened to me, he convinced our ma and da to let him join Senna in her search above the mountain. They must love him beyond measure, even when he was all they had left. I could do with a little of that sort of love. The kind you don't think much about because it's always with you, keeping you warm and safe like a good wool cloak in winter. It's simply *there*, like the strands of wind that play along the floor for you to watch.

Now he's fighting for breath. Sweating through his fancy tunic and hose. Because he wanted to be the hero and find his sister, and the salt and iron were too much for him. I wish I could lay a gentle hand on his heart so I could feel it still beating. Just so I know there's hope.

I kneel, and Senna slings one of Martin's limp arms over my shoulder. He's so flyaway thin that it's no trouble to straighten with him hanging off me like a cloak. I think I can ease us into the pit if he can hold on a little.

A jolt, sharp and sudden, and I'm falling. Senna's holding me by my free arm and then she isn't, and the floor of the wolf pit is rushing at me fast. I scrabble for a handhold and my nails drag down the earthen walls and I try to scream but there's no breath for it, no air.

A flailing shape follows me. Martin is falling, too.

I hit the pit bottom hard. Dizzy white stars everywhere. For the longest moment all I can do is gasp and then . . .

. . . roll slowly, bit by bit, onto my back . . .

. . . and look up, where Senna's face, hovering over the pit, blocking out the pale, tree-scratched sky, is the last thing I see.

I peer over the side of the pit and there she is, sprawled at the bottom like a crumpled handkerchief. Now that it's done, I cannot help but be sorry for her. She asked all the right questions. She had all the right doubts. But she had all the right frailties, too. All the little gaps that let the glamour in.

The boy-thing lies beside her. He will not like the headache that'll greet him when he wakes, but the iron needles I found on the shelf and buried beneath the pallet did their work. All Agnes could see was her sick brother. The urgency of him, how he writhed and suffered.

That part was real. It was hard not to smile.

The trade is complete. A life for a life, by whatever means. There was nothing in the bargain that required me to be truthful.

There's something in my hand. A scrap of green material. It shimmers across my palm, the thousand-thousand greens of fairy cloth catching light that is not there.

It must have torn from his cloak as he fell. It's not in my hand by accident, though. The boy-thing means for me to have it. Even now this wretched scrap of cloth is pitifully trying to make the sky darken, the clouds threaten, the door of the house that is now mine slam in my face. Even now he is trying to foil me, but it's too late and I've held up my end of the bargain. It's been years since the glamour has been able to sway my mind in any meaningful way. Besides, this is the smallest piece of fairy cloth. It could barely make a stone seem like an egg. It will never be able to convince my new ma and da to turn on me when the boy-thing is far away.

I will open my hand. I will throw this scrap of cloth into the pit and leave it there to rot. Taking anything from those fairy wretches always brings the most unintended of consequences.

The cloth flutters between my fingers. The green of it is depthless, and there are so many shades. So many interlocking, intertwining layers of shimmer and gleam.

At the end of this walk will be my new house and this ma and da, my ma and da, and for a while they will want to know where the old Agnes is. They will miss her and weep for her.

I will be the last person who saw her.

When the boy-thing was here, this ma and da breathed in his glamour and saw what he wanted them to see. Thought what he wanted them to think. Now that he's

gone, soon my ma and da will start seeing things as they really are, and they may not like any of it. They may not like me.

There's glamour in this cloth, though. No one to stop me from using it, either.

Ma hugged me. She called me child. *She still may do so after the old Agnes is gone and only I remain. She may do it without the glamour to make her see me as needful and charming. Lovable. Her very own and only.*

She may, but I cannot take that chance. I stuff the scrap of cloak deep into my apron, straighten my skirt, and turn my back on this place one last time.

drag my eyes open. Every last bit of me hurts. I'm damp, too, shoulders to bottom to feet, and there's grit in my hair and my fingertips are aching. I push myself up. My head throbs big—deep—spinny. I'm shivering and it's dark here and I don't like the dark.

Martin. Martin is dying and Senna and I are returning him under the mountain so he gets well. Only I was foolish and slipped and fell into the pit. Senna tried to catch me but she couldn't, and down I went and pulled Martin after me.

I cover my face. I can't bear to see him lying nearby. His neck will be broken. His eyes blank like drying puddles. He was too ill to break his own fall. It will have finished him.

I have to look. If I could face baby Hugh, I can face my own brother.

Slowly I move my hands down. Squint, like that'll make it better somehow, if I see just slivers of his lifeless green body at a time. But there are only dark walls too high to climb and rugged ground where wolves pace and whine and finally meet their ends. No sign of Martin anywhere. No sign of Senna, either, in or out of the pit.

I'm alone.

My arm hair is prickling. Because of Granny I know a little of Those Good People, but it's just enough to keep me wary. It won't help much if I'm to visit the Otherworld. I know they have a kingdom, and there's a king and noble lords and knights and courtiers. I know they feast and revel every night, and they ride on their holy days in an unruly procession through mortal places like Woolpit, and if you know what's good for you, you stay indoors behind salt and iron so you don't interrupt it and earn their wrath. But I know nothing of how to speak to kings and only a little of how to speak to lords. I won't know where to stand in the court. I won't know how to behave.

The safe thing to do is yell for help. Someone in the wheat field will hear me and pull me out. I'll take my thrashing for shirking the harvest and by nightfall I'll have cut-up hands, same as yesterday. The day before that.

But the safe things are all different now. Those Good People do not harm their own. Besides, I promised to get Martin back to his ma and da. If he's—if I can't find— if his body isn't here, the least I can do is tell the king and queen what's befallen him.

I'm finally the girl in the story. Me, Agnes Walter. Even with my dirty feet. My stumbly words. This story will be new. No one will have ever heard one quite like it.

"Senna?" My voice echoes from wall to wall. It does not seem able to climb out and free itself.

The sky overhead is a sickly, faded-out pale with a faint breath of green. Nowhere near the glorious summer blue it should be. It's the color of an old bruise or a day-old corpse. A half-light, as if the sun is going down, but with none of the pinks and oranges of a harvest sunset. The rotty smell is thick, like a drench of cold water.

"Long gone."

I startle and turn around. It's a girl's voice, but not a girl I know, and it's slicey like a sharp knife and amused without being any sort of kind. Martin stumbles out of the shadowy wall of the wolf pit, only it's not Martin. Not exactly. He starts as my brother, but as he weaves toward me, his face gets pointier and his hair longer and his tunic and hose shift and ripple and *change* until he's a girl in a long leaf-colored dress with skin as pale as plaster, and nothing of the green boy remains.

"Wh-what?" I manage, because I'm not sure what I just saw was real and not a story I made up and my head still hurts and if I really did just see Martin turn into a girl, I'm not sure what to say without causing him—her?—offense.

"She's long gone." Not-Martin sways on her feet. "What are you waiting for? Get over here!"

"Oh!" I hurry toward her. She's taller than me now, and heavy in a way the green boy wasn't. She puts all her weight on me and I must stagger. "You look . . . better, at least."

"I will be, now that I'm back here," Not-Martin replies grimly.

"Ah . . . weren't you just a boy? A *green* boy?"

"I only *seemed* to be a boy, and the green was her punishment and not mine. Now walk on and keep quiet. Nothing is worse than foolish questions."

Walk on is what the plowman says to the oxen as he taps their rumps with the guide pole. My face feels hot, like it's just been slapped, but I say nothing as Not-Martin heaves us down a long hallway. And it is a hallway, not the narrow, damp earth walls of the wolf pit. The paneling is made of thousands of tiny twigs woven to make pictures of flowers and butterflies, trees and rivers, stags and boars. The whole place is lit with that greenish light, glowing in ornate holders of . . . saints, is that *gold*?

I'm in the kingdom under the mountain.

Fresh meat, something whispers, and I manage a glance at Not-Martin, but she is whimper-groaning with each shambling step and there are no words in it. We are alone in the corridor; there are no shadows for anything to hide in. Even here, tiny slivers of wind drift in silver swirls along the floor, but when I look up, I can only gape at the glittering bowls of green light high above me, the delicate scrollwork on the arched beams curving toward the ceiling. Not even the manor house is this grand.

"Are we going to see them?" I'm trying to take it all in as we stagger past. "Our ma and da? The king and queen?"

"What part of *nothing is worse than foolish questions* was unclear to you?"

I bite my lip. It's too much like how Glory sounds when I say something she thinks is foolish. Even before the Maying, especially if Kate or Tabby were around, sometimes she'd turn on me this look of everlasting weariness, like *why do I bother?*

I'm not sure how asking about our parents is a foolish question, but I haven't known I'm one of Those Good People for very long and there will be rules for this place, even for a princess. My brother—my *sister*—is sure to help me learn once she feels better.

We turn down a corridor that's dimmer than the others, and the walls are a simple weave of twigs with none of the pictures from the last hallway. My shoulders are aching and my legs afire. Not-Martin stops in front of a plain, sturdy door and waves her hand at it.

Nothing happens.

"Look who's back." One of Those Good People is standing outside the next door down, arms folded,

smug. She looks something like a normal girl, but at the same time . . . *not.* She is lovelier than any mortal girl could ever be, graceful-tall like a cornflower and regal like a warhorse. Her dress is made of—*storm clouds?*—but her voice is all Kate, all Tabby. "If it isn't *Emmmmmrrrrrrrrnnnnthththththth,* who bragged how easy it would be to win her spurs by finishing a job that should have been done long ago."

The name comes out a buzzy drone that doesn't sound like words. She may have been Martin in Woolpit, but now that she is my sister instead of my brother, it seems right to call her by her proper name. Even so, the best I'm going to do is *Em* till I'm better at being one of Those Good People.

Em scowls at the cloud-girl. "*Krrrrrrrshshshshshsh.* I'm in no mood for you. Go away."

"Were you trying to do *this*?" The cloud-girl—Krr—swishes a hand at Em's door and it swings open soundlessly, revealing a spacious chamber with a high ceiling. A plush purple carpet spreads from end to end, and the walls are done up in contrasting shades of green. There's furniture made of wood and gold, and the bed is draped in thick red curtains and piled with heaps of messy, slept-in bedclothes.

This room is as big as the manor house hall. Ten times the size of my home. Yet somehow it's held within the wolf pit, and there must be many others like it.

The Otherworld is a marvel, and I am part of it now.

"Shut up." Em tries to storm into the room but staggers back howling like she walked into a door, one hand pressed to her nose. I catch her, nearly falling on my rump, and when I recover, I reach a hand toward the doorway and gasp when it bumps something solid. Only, nothing is there.

Something giggles. High and shrill, like Kate, like Tabby. I glance all around, bewildered, but it's as if the sound came from the very walls.

Em is hanging off me, barely on her feet, and my shoulder is screaming with holding her up. Krr cackles as Em's pale cheeks grow redder. Just like Glory at the Maying. I pull in a deep breath and do what I should have done then and face Krr and say, "Stop it. Leave her alone. The king won't like how you're speaking to us right now."

Krr's smile widens. "Is it . . . I think it's trying to threaten me."

"No!" I don't know where to look. Anywhere but her face. "Please. Just leave her be."

"Pleeeeeeease," Krr mimics, giggling. "This'll be better than any of us thought. He'll tear them both apart!" She turns on her heel and glides down the corridor, the train of her cloud-gown catching the floor in faint swirls of cold.

Em scowls at me, but weakly, like I'm embarrassing

her somehow. She closes her eyes and scrunches her face, concentrating. When she waves a hand through the empty doorway, there's no barrier, and Em stumbles inside and throws herself in a plush chair piled with wisps of mist that gust everywhichway.

I stand awkwardly in the corridor. I'm not to ask foolish questions. "Ah . . . is it all right if I go find Senna? So you can rest?"

"You can be quiet and make yourself useful. My head is aching." Em puts a hand over her eyes and turns her face into the back of the chair.

I'm not sure what she means by *useful*, so I step into the chamber and my bare feet sink into the soft, thick carpet. It's made of tiny violets, thousands and thousands of them, and they whisper around my toes. This must be Em's room. We must be sharing it. Of course princesses would have a room like this. I really want to meet my ma and da since Senna kept saying how frantic they were to see me, but Em's still clearly not well. I don't know enough about being any kind of princess, much less one of Those Good People, so I'm going to need her help.

There's a small table next to the bed, covered with bowls in tall stacks. I've never seen more than two bowls side by side, except at the manor house when I was invited to eat my fill and get Senna and Martin out from under the table. All that venison, those dishes of savories and mutton glistening in grease—and just like that, a pewter plate appears on the table next to the bowls. On it there's a thick slab of meat covered in rich, velvety sauce.

My mouth waters. I haven't had so much as a sniff of meat since that day.

Eat nothing that's given you, Granny would say, *or you'll never be allowed to leave.*

But I'm the lost princess under the mountain. One meal will do me no harm.

This could be my life. All I must do is choose it. I don't have to go home to Woolpit and that dim, smoky house and the harvest, and all at once the rotty smell rises and here I am in this room, lounging on this bed with this plush red bedcover snug around my ears and I am deciding which of my gowns I'll wear because there's a feast in my honor and so many people want to know what I think and hang on every word of the stories I tell—

The pig bite on my leg stings, a solid stab that makes me buckle. It's not healing like it should. Mayhap it will, now that I'm in the Otherworld where I belong.

I'm turning back to the meat, eager for that first juicy bite, when a wolf appears sleek and silent in the open doorway. There's no cover. Nothing to duck behind. I screech and grip the meat knife, but it's not a knife anymore. It's a stick, the kind you'd throw for a dog to fetch.

The kind a small child would use to play swords. I reach for the meat to throw to him, only there's nothing but moss on a slab of tree bark.

My whole leg throbs. That wolf will devour me and leave my bones to bleach.

The wolf doesn't growl or lunge. He just stands there until Em rolls her head enough to get a look at him. Then she winces, mutters a curse, and hauls herself to her feet, but she isn't two steps from her chair before she sways hard and falls to her knees.

"Tell him I'm indisposed!" Em shouts at the wolf. "Tell him I'll present myself before the court when I've had a chance to bathe and change."

The wolf cocks his head.

"Ugh, very well, fine." Em waves a hand at me where I'm standing frozen, openmouthed, helplessly clutching a stick that should be a knife. "Help me up."

She said *before the court*. We must finally be going to see our ma and da. The story will go like this: I will walk into the throne room and the king and queen will know me on sight. They will rise from their places as one, weeping openly, *you are our baby*, and they will hold out their arms and I will hug them. They'll be able to tell me what just happened with the meat and the knife, why those things disappeared and left sticks and moss in their places. I'll tell them how my Woolpit ma and da raised me with love and kindness, how they ought to be rewarded for it. I'll tell them what good work Senna did finding me and explaining everything and they will give her the room next to this one. It would be nice to have a friend nearby.

I will visit my old parents in the village. I can help them once I learn to magic things. Any Woolpit ma who has something mean to say will find her cat refusing to hunt and her house overrun with mice. The May King just might fall in a mudhole. Once Glory knows, she's sure to forgive me, and I'll help her, too, and watch over all the babies so nothing bad happens to one of them again.

I help Em up and arrange her arm over my shoulder. She has more of her footing now and shuffles along mostly of her own power. Her cheeks are pinker and she's muttering how someone will pay, although I must be mishearing because I'm doing her a kindness. The corridor is grand and high and lit with that faint greenish light. Higher than the manor house, and grander, too, but ominous where the manor house was cheerful. This is a place of dark corners. A place of forgetting.

Go ahead, try to run, something whispers. *We'll be waiting.*

"What is that?" I ask. "Who's saying that?"

Em makes no reply and hauls me into a bigger, airier hallway with huge spidery fixtures marching down the ceiling, each holding hundreds of glowing green leaves.

She's shambling us toward a towering doorway made of bright gold, shining on its own despite the green light dimming it down. It's set with jewels the size of my two hands together. My heart is racing because I'm going to stand before the king under the mountain, who is also my first da, and I haven't had a chance to plan what I want to say.

Just outside the doorway, Em drags her arm off my shoulders, closes her eyes, and mutters something. That leaf-rot smell hits me hard enough that I choke and everything goes fuzzy. I blink, and Em is walking alone into the room, limping the smallest bit. I hurry in behind her. This is a court and there must be rules, but this is also my ma and da. I am their baby in a way I've never been anyone else's.

The chamber is a sitting room of some sort. The floor is made of light and dark stones worked in alternating squares. It's sprawling and airy, and there are chairs and settees made of plump moss, and Those Good People are sitting in them, or standing near them, so many and so scary-beautiful that for a long moment I wonder how I can be one of them, round and pink like I am with too many freckles. A murmur goes through the room as we enter, followed by whispering and then snort-laughs.

There are others here. This reunion should be private.

At the far end of the room is a man sitting in a massive chair that seems to be carved from a single block of gold. His feet are propped on a blue cushion set on a wooden stool. He has long dark hair in graceful ringlets, and his tunic is a shimmering array of greens that's a thousand-thousand times richer than Senna's. I've never seen anyone so beautiful.

This is the king under the mountain. He can be no other.

My ears are roaring. This is my da. My first da, who's been worried for me since I got lost all those years ago, who sent Senna to bring me home. I don't see the queen. My ma. He's alone, no one within an arm's length, and Em is moving straight toward him, trying to walk steady on and not limp or sway. The room is pin-drop quiet, but Those Good People are grinning, fighting down laughter, and I cannot think what's funny. This moment will be touching and joyous.

Em kneels. She's breathing hard, through her teeth. Still ailing from being above the mountain, likely. The king barely looks at us. At my sister and me. So I kneel as well. One day we will laugh about this, how his lost baby appeared before him on her knees like any common subject.

"You failed to present yourself when you arrived," the king says to Em. "I had to send for you. I should not have to send for you."

"Beg pardon, sire." Em lurches to her feet, unsteady and weak.

"Is something the matter with you?"

Em shakes her head, and there's a ripple throughout the room as Those Good People snicker behind their graceful hands.

"You're not ill?" The king looks concerned, but in a mocking way, like Kate, like Tabby. "Not, say, ironsick from where a mortal girl buried two crossed needles beneath your bed?"

That cannot be right. I hid those needles well so they'd cause no harm. Besides, Senna would never do such a thing and no other girls have come near our house.

"I'm fine, sire," Em says, making a stiff curtsy. "Come to claim what's due me."

"What's *due* you?" The king raises a brow. "This isn't the mortal thing you left with."

"No, this one is better." She kicks me till I rise, then shoves me forward. "Go on. Go hug your daddy."

The king isn't smiling. His beautiful brown face is set like a cat tracking prey. "What is this thing doing here? Do you think this is funny somehow?"

Em blinks rapidly. "Sire. It's . . ."

The room is spinning, slow and sickening, and for the first time since Senna spoke the words, it dawns on me what being the lost princess under the mountain well and truly means. Those Good People are pitiless and cruel, and I will have to live among them. They delight in trickery and malice for the mere sake of it, and they have no patience for foolishness or idleness or greed. They take what isn't theirs, if they can get away with it, and nothing they have is real.

In Woolpit I have a ma and da. They are real. They are kind, even if they're dull, and I want to be back there with them. Right now. Cut-up hands and porridge and everything.

"Pardon me," I say, and my voice cracks but I can't stop now. "Milord. Sire. I—"

"I wager *Emmmmmmrrrrrrrrrnnnnnthththththth* was dragging her feet presenting herself here because she hopes we won't recall her last disastrous mistake." A young man who looks much like the king leans gracefully over the back of a chair and aims a mean Tabby-smile at Em. "It's one thing to turn one of these servant-things into a more useful creature. Quite another to lose track of it."

Em whirls, her hands in fists. "You laughed like everyone else. And that creature is still here somewhere."

The king sits up straighter. "If this isn't the girl-thing you left with, then she won the bargain."

Precious few things gain and hold attention in the Otherworld, Granny would say. *One is a bargain. The other is a sacrifice.*

"If she won the bargain," he goes on, "it means the

girl-thing made a fool of me. After you swore up and down she'd fail. You'd see to it, you said. She'd never be able to face a boy the image of her dead brother, and she'd fall apart. You *swore* this." He narrows his eyes. "Then again, you swore once that she'd never so much as think about the crossing place again."

Em looks worse than sick now, but she stands proud like a stalk of wheat. I can't breathe. He's talking about Senna. There can be no other *thing* he means.

"Instead a mortal girl bested my conditions and won her freedom," the king growls, "and you have the cheek to turn up here, before every last one of my court, and you're not kneeling and cowering with the shame of it?"

"There is this one." Em's voice trembles. "Blood must serve. This one has the blood. What difference is it?"

This isn't right. This *can't* be right. A princess doesn't serve. A princess wears pretty dresses. She eats meat and honey cake instead of beans and porridge. She is the girl in the story.

"There is every difference and you know it." The king's face is hard, his voice a terrible kind of calm. "This one here can't help that she's brainless. But you?" He levels a finger at Em. "If you know what's good for you, you will get out of my sight and be very, very careful when you next come into it."

Em backs away slowly. I cannot move. I'm alone in the huge, airy chamber with the tall ceiling beams and the eerie green light and Those Good People smirking openly from the edges of the room.

"What are you still doing here?" The king frowns at me.

"I came to see my ma and da," I whisper, but it carries like my normal voice and sets the whole court howling with laughter. "The king and queen under the mountain. I came because Senna said I was the lost princess and I wandered away and you wanted me to come home. So we could be a family."

"To think," the king says to no one in particular, "that mortal girl went out of her way to cripple *Emmmmmrrrrrrrrnnnnnthththththth* just so she wouldn't interfere, when all along this halfwit thing believed every word."

Em is alive and recovering and back where she belongs, just like I promised. I have no more reason to be here. No more wish to. "Please. I brought back your child who was sick. Where is Senna? She said I could go home to Woolpit whenever I liked."

"My *child*? You mean—" The king under the mountain barks a long, echoing laugh that cracks like thunder amid the giggling court. "*Emmmmmmrrrrrrrrrnnnnnthththththth*, my child. I'd have drowned her years ago if it were so. At least you are amusing. The other mortal girl was too dour and frowny."

"S-Senna?" I choke. "Please, I just want to go home."

"I imagine she said a lot of things to get you down here," the king replies. "That was the bargain, after all. A life for a life, traded by whatever means. Now you are here and here you'll stay. Blood must serve. If not hers, then yours."

"No," I whisper, because it's hitting me in waves that I'm in the worst kind of story. The kind you tell yourself can't be true because its ending is unthinkable.

The king leans back on his throne and makes a little shooing motion. "I'm bored. Go away."

I'm frozen. Wavery and weak. Senna could lie to me because she is not one of Those Good People. She never was. She's a girl like me. She was the girl in her own story, and she has gotten the happy ending.

Something dark and furry twines around my ankles. It's a rat and it's as long as my arm and I shriek and kick it and it goes tumbling and screeeeeeing across the black-and-white floor.

If Senna is not one of Those Good People, none of what she told me is true. It's never been true. I'm not the lost princess. There'll be no dancing. No feasting. No people paying me mind, caring what I think.

Laughter all around me. Those Good People are snickering and cackling and guffawing, not bothering to hide it behind their hands any longer, but doubled over and holding their bellies. Their stark, lovely faces swarm and blur. I am like Glory at the Maying, only it's worse because at least she could run home and hide under her bedclothes and cry.

I have nowhere to go, and it's no one's fault but my own. I was fool enough to listen to a story and believe every word.

become her with every step. Across the heath, and I am Agnes. Past the mill, Agnes. By the time I climb the little rise and my house comes in view, my yard and my fence and my garden, there was never any other Agnes but me.

Past the threshold, past the fire, to the sackcloth bag hanging from the rafters. There is bread inside, suspended here to keep the mice away, and my hands are trembling so hard I can barely work the knot. Then it crumbles out and into my hands and I shove the lot into my mouth.

Then I wait. Palms slick. Heart racing.

I do not die.

Instead the crumbs go soft on my tongue, soggy and nutty with the tiny odd stone from the mill, and I sob, nearly choking, because it means the whole business is behind me now. There were conditions, and this was one of them. The food under the mountain no longer has any hold on me. I have escaped the fair folk. I am a girl

again. I am a girl with a ma and a da and a home and a sky to be under. I am this girl now. I am Agnes, and she is me. She is what's left of Senna, daughter of Duro and Oconea. She just might be the last of the Trinovantes who walked this place so long ago that even the land does not remember us.

A shadow falls across the doorway. Everyone is still at the harvest and I reach for the iron needles that remain buried in the dirt beneath her—my—sleeping pallet. The fair folk have no more claim on me. That was the bargain.

It's not one of those fairy wretches, though. It's the pig.

She stands in the doorway making a low, throaty sound like I'm the one who doesn't belong here. I scratch the needles out of the ground. An angry pig who outweighs you thrice-over is nothing to ignore. Slowly I move around the fire to study her. The old Agnes spoke to this pig like she was a friend. Mother, she's called.

We should all be so lucky to have more than one mother.

Mother is glaring at me. There's no other word for it. She makes that rumbly sound a few more times, then swings her rear end around and relieves herself in a stinking pile right on the threshold. Then she lumbers past the shed out of sight, and I'm left to clean up the mess.

It's like she thinks to punish me.

After I put supper on the fire, I sit in the yard and run my hands over the dirt. We would meet here for the shearing. None of these houses stood then. Neither the paths nor the mill, and definitely not the abbey and its everclanging bells. We would meet here, Trinovantes from everywhere in a day's walk, and sometimes a few Iceni would come down through the woods. My first da would sharpen the shears and my first ma would choose a lamb to roast for the feast. My brother would pull my hair and I would chase him, ready to pounce and tickle.

This spot, beneath my hands. It's nothing like it was, but it is still here.

The sun is going down when I spot Ma and Da coming up the hill from the wheat field. I rub my thumb against the fairy cloth in my apron. They are so used to the boy-thing's glamour that they will not notice more. I fly down the path and greet them both with deep, long hugs. They hug me back, and they don't let go until I do.

We sit down to supper. The three of us share the bench near the fire, and I savor bite after bite of porridge.

"Something is missing," Da says.

"We had guests here," Ma replies. "Fosterlings."

I press a hand over the green cloth in my apron, but carefully, because too much and they will be glamourstruck. Too much and they will go mad.

Da shrugs. "They must have gone back where they belong."

There's no need for it, but I keep my hand near the cloth well after they begin to discuss how much longer the harvest will last. No more is said of the fosterlings. Agnes has always been their very own and only.

The throne room is a gut-lurch blur. Those Good People are still laughing. I can't stay here. I turn and crack heads with someone, and I stumble back whimpering because if I've just collided with one of Those Good People, I'm worse than dead. But it's not. It's a girl. A normal girl, whisper-thin with chapped lips and a crooked nose, a few summers older than me. She's cradling the rat I kicked and staring at me with eyes like moons.

"Oh, gods," breathes the girl. "She did it. Senna actually did it."

Her look is part pitying and part sad, but her stooped-over cringe is all fear as she pulls me with her toward a rat-size hole in a shadowy corner. I let her lead me. Head down, eyes blurry, belly awash with sick. Squares of black-and-white floor stone flash beneath my feet. I duck my head to move through the hole that is suddenly our size, and abruptly the floor becomes rough, uneven ground. It's dark here, and damp, and lit with that greenish light that's starting to give me a headache. My chest feels full of hot, wet wool, but I'm shivering.

Go ahead and cry, something whispers. *We like it when you cry.*

"I'm Acatica," the girl says as we move down a narrow, musty corridor made of rough-hewn stone. The rat lies in the crook of her arm like a baby. "Do you understand me? If you don't, breathe in deep. Like this. The glamour should work its way into your ears soon enough and we'll understand each other however we speak."

Too much is happening too quickly. I'm not the lost princess under the mountain. Senna lied to me. I'm never going home.

"You can sit here, but only for a moment." Acatica settles me on a knee-high stone next to the damp wall. She steps away and holds the rat in the light, running gentle hands down its legs and along its belly.

I could have paid some heed to all those things that were the way I wanted them to be instead of the way they were. I know the stories. I should have seen it. I close my eyes and lean against the wall and hug myself tight.

Get off, something growls, and I leap forward because something *stings* me, too, sharp and cruel across both shoulders. I swivel, rubbing the hurt through my dress, but there's only bare wall. No spiders or wasps or insects of any kind.

Acatica is still looking the rat over. Finally, satisfied it's not hurt, she stoops and lets it go. It scurries into the shadows and disappears, its little claws ticking on the stone. Then she turns to me. "Be kind to them, understand? They're already paying a price. And when one of them comes to fetch you, by all means go."

"Fetch me? Fetch me where?" I shiver. "I'm not following a rat anywhere."

"That's how our masters summon us," Acatica replies, "and do not even *jest* about refusing to do what you're told."

They snatch away the curious, Granny would say. *They take the rude and the greedy and the vicious, and every now and then they snatch away the innocent, just because they can. Just to remind us that there is truly no such thing.*

"Every night our masters revel," Acatica says. "They'll pack that hall from one end to the other and they will feast till dawn. There will need to be food and drink, lots of it, and each of them will need a new gown, or a tunic trimmed with moonlight, or the shiniest, pointiest boots. It all must be ready at the appointed time."

She gives me a long look that fills in the *or else* hanging at the end, but the way she says it, the way it comes together in my head—it's a story. This is the part of the story where the girl has an impossible task, and she must complete it or be eaten by the monster or married off to the foul prince or cast into the sea to drown. But if I'm the girl in the story, it means there's a way through. It means there's a way to get to *the end* with me safe in Woolpit and Senna punished for her treachery.

"The passageways are all unguarded," I tell her. "Nothing's stopping us. We can make a run for it. Right now."

Acatica sighs. "There's no need for guards. The walls dislike us, and they'll only toy with us before trapping us somewhere or humming a tune till we're mad or just forcing us to wander in circles till we fall down as a pile of bones. The last thing they'll do is heed us."

"The walls . . . can think for themselves?"

"Don't touch them, either. They don't like being touched. They'll leave you alone if you leave them alone, and do as you're bidden."

The whispering. It's been coming from the *walls*. I shudder and rub the welts on my shoulders. "There has to be a way."

"I thought so too." Acatica smiles sadly. "For a while. Lots of us did. They're not around anymore, though."

She nods at the walls and I go cold all over.

"Senna got away," I reply. "If she escaped, so can I. So can *we*."

"No. Senna made a trade. Your life for hers." Acatica gestures for me to stand and leads me down the corridor. "She made a bargain with the king, that if she could find someone to take her place who shared her blood, she would be free."

"But we don't share blood. How can we? She's . . . well, she's green."

"The green is a punishment," Acatica says. "Like a branding. Senna went too many times to the crossing place, so they marked her as their own. To remind her. She looked like you once. Like me. Like all the Trinovantes who agreed to serve under the mountain."

"You *agreed* to this?" I jerk back. "Who in their right mind would possibly do such a thing? Didn't you know the stories? Or did you just not heed them?"

"Did I know the stories?" Acatica snorts a laugh. "Who do you think made them? Who do you think *lived* them?"

I trail to a stop in a pool of greenish light.

"Our people," Acatica goes on. "We were Trinovantes. The ones who lived. We are the stories. They were all we could give you. We whispered our stories into the flowers. We shouted them into stones. Sometimes they made it up to you, to the people above the mountain. Some of you we managed to save."

There are thousands of stories in thousands of places. It's not every day you stand before one of them.

"We are not Trinovantes in Woolpit," I reply slowly, and I struggle to match her pace as she moves down the passageway.

"No. Trinovantes are gone now." Acatica turns a

corner. "Some tried to run. Most chose to stay. To fight those foreign soldiers, for all the good it did. We were dying when the king under the mountain made us a bargain. Serve him and live. I took it. So did Senna. We were friends then. Here?" She makes a bleak gesture to the walls, the light, the shadows. "It's the first thing you lose."

"That's not much of a bargain," I say.

Acatica shrugs and rounds another corner. "No, of course not. Even in the moment we all knew exactly what sort of creatures we were agreeing to serve. But when you see . . . *things* . . . you go numb. You do whatever it takes to make them stop. Later, when you can think again, sometimes you don't even recognize the person you've become. But it's done. There's no going back."

"Senna did." I can't keep the poison out of my voice. "She got back."

"She shouldn't have." Acatica smiles, dim and sad. "The king set up conditions so she was sure to fail. There'd be no one left, you see. That was the only reason the king agreed to let her try. She'd fail, and watching her fail would amuse the whole court. What befell her when she was snatched back would make the rest of us think twice before daring to approach the king under the mountain with any foolish notions."

"But she didn't fail," I whisper, and I blink back angry tears. "How can she even stay? She must have eaten the food under the mountain."

"To remain among her kind, Senna had to fulfill all conditions of the bargain. Someone with her blood had to take her place, and she could never speak of where she'd been to anyone, for any reason. If she managed it, all things tethering her to the Otherworld would have no more hold. Even having eaten the food."

I think of the meat in Em's chamber, how close I came to sliding that knife through it and taking a bite, and I shiver. I'm sure to be tempted again. I'll have to keep my wits about me or I'll never be allowed to leave.

Those Good People honor a bargain, Granny would say, *but they also hate to lose. That is why you never, never agree to anything they say, even when it seems like all will work out to your benefit.*

I follow Acatica toward a glowing doorway. The room we enter is small, about the size of a house in Woolpit, and it's lined on three sides with trestle tables. It's warm and damp here, like hiding beneath the bedclothes and breathing your own breath. The room is filled with kids, all with their backs to me, crowded shoulder to shoulder doing some kind of work at the tables.

"I know you've just been given quite a blow," Acatica says as she leads me toward the table at the far end of the room, "but we cannot have anyone standing idle. Hand work will be the best task for you."

The table is piled with leaves, sticks, moss, and lichen. The kinds of things you'd rake out of the corners of the yard and pile on top of the garden to help it winter over. The girl at my right is weaving crumbly brown leaves into platters. Or rather, she's holding the leaves near one another and they're weaving *themselves*, stems twining into a tight spiral like they grew there on purpose.

"They've been glamoured, see?" Acatica says. "Glamour makes one thing seem like another. We can't command it like our masters, but we can direct it if it's already there. If it's not redirected by someone more powerful. Here, you try it."

I pull a handful of leaves from the pile. The kids at my table are working so fast it's hard to follow what they're doing. Acatica joins them. Platters pile up, all different sizes in neat stacks. Row after row of mugs made of twigs. I touch the stems of two bright oak leaves together, and sure enough, they curve around tight and cling so hard I can't tug them apart.

"Good." Acatica looks up from forming moss into compact balls and piling them in a basket made of weedy stems. She smiles like Glory used to when we'd make flower crowns all afternoon, and I miss flower crowns and I miss Glory. Or rather, I miss the Glory who loved making flower crowns all afternoon and didn't half-heartedly twine a dandelion or two before complaining how the flowers stained her fingers.

I miss the Glory who'd see me struggling and wait for

me to line up words, to learn the task, to get the rules of the game. Who'd make other people wait. Who'd stand close and whisper *take your time* while I babbled and stumbled.

I start on a platter. Leaf by leaf. Some I have to do over because however I'm directing the glamour doesn't make the stems tight enough. Around me, kids work feverishly, each turning out ten plates by the time my first one is finished.

"Splendid!" Acatica says. "Put it on the pile, then keep going."

"How many do we need to make?" I ask.

"Just keep working."

"But Those Good People won't want to eat off dishes made of leaves!"

Acatica smirks. "Don't worry. The dishes are well glamoured. As far as our masters are concerned, they're eating off silver and gold. They might not be able to make something out of nothing, but they can make nothing *seem* like something."

Those Good People can make nothing of their own. They need human hands to do their work.

"What if we decide we're not doing work for them anymore?"

She tips her chin at the massive rat that's making its way along the table through the platters and leaves.

"But it . . . it just *seems* like a rat, right?" My mouth

feels stuffed with yard waste. "It's still a person. Right?"

"Only birth and death can stop the seeming," Acatica says, "unless one of our masters decides to take the glamour off."

My hands go still. I should never have kicked one. Doesn't cost a penny to be kind. Especially when you don't know what you're dealing with.

The rat stops in front of Acatica, sits on its hind-quarters, and goes *screeeeeee*. She stiffens, then pushes away from the table and follows as the rat skitters toward the door.

"What am I to do?" I ask, but what I really want to say is *don't leave me here alone.*

"Keep working," Acatica says over her shoulder, and she's gone.

I do. I'm glad none of the other kids feels much like talking. Every now and then someone comes to collect the things we've made. The leaves and twigs are dry. They slice my hands. It's like the wheat field, cuts atop cuts, only this time I'm nowhere near my da and I sure wish I was. I fall into a rhythm. I weave and twist and twine and fold. It feels like days. It feels like months. It can't be, though, and soon enough whoever is reeve here will blow his horn and we can stop. We can sleep.

My fingers sting. I pause long enough to flex them and choke on a scream. They're stumps, ground down below the knuckle and too raw to even bleed.

"It only seems," I whisper, "it only seems."

I tell it to myself like a story, because I badly need something to believe.

I wake up in Agnes's bed. I eat Agnes's breakfast. Ma runs her fingers through my hair and I snuggle next to her on the hearth bench and close my eyes and in the darkness there, it's like coming home. It doesn't need to be the same. It only needs to be enough.

The reeve turns up at the door each morning, calling villagers to the harvest. Ma and Da insist I'm still recovering from my ordeal. The reeve gives me a long, measuring glance, but he does not overrule them. I rub the fairy cloth nestled deep in my apron, and he does not ask about the old Agnes. He does not ask where the boy-thing has gotten to.

I keep Agnes's fire. I weed her garden and sweep her floor and set scraps out for her pig, even if it does not like me and rarely comes into the yard now that Agnes is gone. At last the harvest is in, and now I can win Agnes's friends.

It won't be long before everything that belonged to

Agnes becomes mine, and the girl who once was Agnes was never really here.

I pack a basket with some mending and walk down the path through the village. It's still uncanny to see so many houses this close together, but soon I'm standing before the place where the golden-headed fluffwit lives.

There are two iron needles tacked crosswise on her door.

This house is nicer than the one I live in. The thatch gleams in the autumn sun, and the wattled walls don't have a single crack. The walk has been swept and there are herbs in rows within easy reach of the door. The old Agnes could not stop talking about this girl, but I remember Glory Miller best from the pit, how much noise she made about finding us and saving us with nary a mention of anyone else.

Still. If she and Agnes are friends, there must be something to her.

Glory is standing under the eave of the house, trying to work her way into a yoke. The dangling buckets crack her knees and she curses. She sees me coming and frowns like she recognizes me somehow but cannot recall from where.

"Want some help?" I smile and nod at the tangled buckets.

Glory's mouth falls open. "You can talk?"

"I've always been able to talk."

"You've always been able to talk," she repeats, like she

was foolish for believing anything else. "Ah. Hello. I'm Glory."

"Agnes." I rub the cloth and direct this girl, clear and firm, to know it, to believe it, to say it.

At length Glory replies dreamily, "Yes. Agnes."

"And we are friends," I go on, releasing the cloth and reaching for one of the ropes. "You are friends with Agnes. Here, shift that crosspiece so it's even over your shoulders."

"Ohhh, but Agnes is a liar," Glory grumbles. "Always making things up so she'll seem important. Never thinking how people don't like being fooled."

"Well, there'll be no more of that." I step back from her, the buckets now dangling properly at either end of the yoke. "I have no interest in stories."

"Ah." Glory smiles halfway. "I'm off, then. Ma's sent me for water."

"Don't you want me to come with you?" I ask, and I give her the answer so clear that all she must do is nod.

Glory looks bewildered. "Not particularly. Please yourself, though."

I wait, but Glory merely steadies her buckets and waves a clumsy farewell. We should be shoulder to shoulder by now, arms linked and giggling. She is . . . resisting in some way. I frown and gently tap the cloth once more. "I'm happy to help."

"You're happy to help," Glory says, but then she blinks

oddly and starts fidgeting under the yoke, trying to balance buckets that already hang even.

This is not right, but I dare not nudge her again. I don't want her to be glamourstruck, and I also have no idea how much is left in this little scrap of cloth. I must use it well.

A woman in her middle years appears in the doorway. Her hair is covered, but she and Glory both have broad foreheads and eyes the same blue as a bird egg. The moment she sees me, the woman straightens like an apprentice caught idle. "You—you're not—ah. Good morning, Green Agnes. I . . . ah . . . you're here. Near my house. Somehow."

"Green Agnes," Glory echoes, and she squints and sees me, and I whip a glare at Glory's ma for disrupting my glamour.

Glory's ma steps outside and closes the door tight behind her. The iron needles clank faintly. She stands sturdy like she'd challenge me to a fight, only her face is gray, her lip trembling. "Is the green boy with you? Can't imagine what might bring you by. There hasn't been a baby here for months."

She is not sure what I am. She thinks to ward me away with salt and iron at her threshold. Little wonder the glamour is haphazard.

I fight to keep my look pleasant. Already Glory is frowning, like she's not seeing Agnes anymore, yet I am Agnes. I have to be. "Beg your pardon, mistress, and please hear this nice, but I have no liking for babies."

"That's close enough." Glory's ma doesn't exactly say it to me; rather, she says it in my direction, in a scratchy, singsong voice. "The windows and doors are well secured. There's nothing here for either you or the boy."

Salt and iron disrupt whatever mischief the creatures under the mountain intend. They'd rant about it for days. There were houses they couldn't enter, children they could not grab, simply because there was a poker at a yard gate or salt sewed into a hem.

I move away from the doorstep. Just being close to this house might strip away whatever glamour still clings to the cloth in my apron.

"Yes, where is your brother?" Glory looks like a misshapen beast, hunched with the yoke across her shoulders. "I've not seen him anywhere since the harvest."

"He's always been sickly," I reply, and I rub the cloth harder against the force of the iron needles on the door. "He stays close to home."

Glory's ma lifts her pale brows. "Does he? Must be nice for Matilda, having a son again. Some of us may never know that joy. Others of us don't deserve it."

I narrow my eyes. That is Ma she's slandering. Then I soften, because she must be the ma of the baby that the old Agnes wept over. Those fairy wretches did not snatch him away, though I see why Glory's ma wants to think it. Sometimes it helps mend grief, having someone to blame who cannot be punished or touched.

"Go back to your place," says Glory's ma, and she does not mean my house. "The rest of us want no trouble from you."

The rest of us. She says it pleasant, but there's something of a threat deep within. If I am to stay, if I am to be Agnes and grow old here, this village cannot keep seeing me as the green girl. It's not enough for me to win Agnes's friends.

I must win her whole village as well.

creeeeeeee.

S I'm awake in a heartbeat and scramble away from the rat by my knee. *Awake* is the wrong word. I'm slumped in a heap on the workroom floor. I haven't been sleeping. It's like I've been put away, like a needle or a hoof pick or a doll you're finished play-ing with. I push myself up and then panic because my fingers—

Are back. Entirely the way they were not a day ago. They're not even raw and red.

The rat is screeing, scampering impatiently between me and the door like it's in a hurry somehow. Like it's anxious.

Most of the other girls are folded over too, likely where they collapsed after all those hours making things out of yard waste. A few are listlessly working stray leaves and bark shavings into slices of meat and slabs of honey cake. My belly rumbles, but I know better

than to eat anything here. Acatica is nowhere in sight, and I hope it's because she has somewhere nice to sleep and not because she's this rat trying like mad to get me to follow it.

The rat shambles ahead. I keep to the middle of the corridors beneath the spindly ceiling fixtures. I want no trouble with the walls. There's the safe thing and then there's the smart thing. The rat stops in front of a door that seems familiar and chirrs at me till I knock.

Em throws the door open. She frowns as if I'm late, then makes a come-here gesture like you would to a dog. "Hurry. I've got an audience with the king."

She buzzes away toward a footrest piled with heaps of mist and sunlight and dew, but I'm frozen in the hallway. Just looking at her makes me feel small and foolish. The kind of numbwit who's easy to trick.

"Well?" She's impatient, sunk to the ankles in that lush carpet of violets.

I grit my teeth. After all she's done, for her to think I'll just turn up and help her. But the rat at my feet screes at me again, like it's telling me I'd better do as I'm told.

"I'm going to wear my glowworm gown." Em puts herself on a little stool in front of her dressing table and starts magicking butterflies into her hair like pins. She looks stronger. Whatever sickness Senna gave her must have passed. "Get it."

She's not even going to help. She's not even going to turn around and look at me.

I scowl as I step into the room and search for something that might be a glowworm dress. There are heaps of leaves and lichens everywhere, like a compost heap sneezed, but no dresses. Nothing that could even be mistaken for a dress, but behind a coffer I find a nest of glowworms in a writhing, shining mass.

They can make nothing for themselves. That's why they need us.

These little creatures were a gown at one point. Now they're glowworms again. Everything here was once clothing, and now it's yard waste.

I gently scoop up a handful of glowworms and work them as I did the leaves. It isn't difficult, but there are hundreds and each must be convinced to curl next to its friends in the shape of a bodice and sleeves and skirts. Beneath my fingers, the glowworms brighten and fade, brighten and fade. On summer nights in Woolpit, Glory and I would find them in the undergrowth and we'd each collect a palmful just to watch them make light in their wondrous tails.

Only this summer Glory kept her distance, still fuming, and I had to find them myself. Then she started speaking to me, little one-word answers along with lots of weary sighs like her ma insisted she be courteous, only she kept having things to do so she couldn't go

glowworm hunting. One night I spotted her near a little fire. I had a palmful to show her, but when I got near, she and Kate and Tabby were playing one of those predict-your-future-husband games, exploding apples in the coals—as if Glory is anywhere old enough for courting. She saw me coming over their heads and gave me such a fierce look that I backed away, cupping my hand over the poor little worms so my running home wouldn't cause them to fall.

When the gown is finished, I gingerly carry it to the dressing table and ease it open so Em can step in. The little creatures part amiably and then cling together down her pale back snugger than any lacings.

"Can I go?" I must find Acatica. To make sure she's all right, and also because just being near her makes this place much less dark.

"Not yet. I need you to carry my train. Keep still." Em holds her hand palm up and blows a fine sand into my face. That rotty, dead-leaf smell hits like a fist and I stagger back, snuffling the grit out of my nose, swiping at my eyes, fighting down a choke as it coats the back of my throat. The pig bite on my leg hurts in deep, throbby stabs.

Em peers at me. "That'll do. It's a bit of a hash-job, but it can't be helped."

I'm almost afraid to look down, but when I do— squinting, just in case it's worse than I thought—my tattery shift dress has somehow become a plain but elegant gown, apron, and matching hose, all woven of the tiniest of tiny twigs. It's almost like kindness so I try to say thank you, only it comes out as a long, screeching donkey bray.

I slap a hand over my mouth. It's worse than words coming out all confusing and jumbled, and Em cackles Kate-like before flouncing a long cloud of meadow mist near her shoulders.

"Hold that off the floor." Em heads for the hallway. "It's delicate, and if it gets torn, there will be consequences. I can hardly appear before the king without it, though."

I sweep the mist into my arms and hurry after Em. As I handle it, the mist becomes a graceful train, weaving its way into the glowworm gown and sinking deep. It's cool and gentle on my hands, swirling constantly, a lovely gray blue with the smallest sheen of purple. We move along corridors until Em stops abruptly in front of a small room lined with sheer panes of crystal. The king under the mountain is standing with his back to the door, leaning over a basin made from a gem that's perched on a slim, graceful pedestal. He's facing a still, clear pool of water set in the wall that reflects his likeness. He peers at himself, tilting his head this way and that, hovering a golden blade near his bristly brown cheek.

Only yesterday the king told Em to think very carefully about when next she appeared before him. And yet here she is. Here *I* am. The girl Senna tricked, whose trickery makes the king look like a fool.

Or was it yesterday? It feels as if it must be, yet it feels timeless, too. Both and neither.

"Sire." Em clears her throat and the king tenses. He closes his eyes, breathes out long and windy like a horse, then touches his blade to his cheek a few more times, but slowly and without intention.

At last he turns, glances at Em, then picks up a leaf to wipe his blade. "Are you so desperate for an audience? How sad."

"No. Well, yes." Em's voice goes careful and measured. "Sire, there's been a mistake. With the revel tonight. The seating order."

My hands and arms are now tiny panes of crystal that blend seamlessly with the walls. My hem and feet are stones, same as the floor. I bite back a scream, then hesitantly flex my fingers, praying they won't shatter. Bits of the dust Em blew on me fall from the hair-thin cracks in my hands and drift toward the ground on a silver whisper of wind.

It only seems. It's not real.

I hope.

"Has there?" The king turns back to the mirror and fidgets with his chin. The golden blade catches light and winks. "Take it up with my steward. He makes all those sorts of arrangements."

"I did." Em's voice is brittle and too polite. "I'm in the fifty-first row. The *fifty-first*! I've never been lower than the thirtieth."

"Oh, that's definitely a mistake," the king replies to his likeness. "I told him nothing better than row seventy."

"I've done nothing to deserve this." Em means it to sound firm, to appeal to some sense of fairness, but there's a waver deep in it and her neck is turning bright berry red. "What happened with the girl-thing is not my fault."

"Interesting that you should bring up fault." The king scrapes the blade just above his beard, tidying the line of it. "My son made an interesting point at the revel last night, which unfortunately you did not hear because your row was still waiting for permission to enter."

Em scowls but says nothing. The butterflies in her hair gently fan their wings.

"The Crown Prince wondered why the mortal girl was able to summon anyone at all to trade with. He pointed out, rightfully, that every numbwit hapless thing with that blood was either long dead or serving under the mountain." The king meets Em's eyes in the watery looking glass. "That was what made it amusing."

"I'm sure the Crown Prince has many interesting ideas that are entirely his own and not put there by those who would kiss his . . . ring." Em makes a small, polite gesture that is also somehow mocking. "He does love that jibberjab about the pig."

"Jibberjab, is it?" the king asks quietly. "Right, then deny it. Deny you turned one of the mortal things into a pig and now you don't know where it's gotten to."

A pig loose in the court under the mountain would serve Those Good People right. Pigs are not splendid and elegant like everything else here. Pigs bump tables hard enough to knock food on the floor, then gobble it down while you try to shove them clear.

"Begging your pardon, sire, but do *you* know where every servant under the mountain is at this very moment?"

The king turns his attention back to his likeness in the pool-mirror. "My son wondered whether the pig escaped somehow, and this girl-thing right now holding up a train that you have no right to wear is that very pig."

Em buzzes something low and angry. Whatever she did to keep me from being seen obviously didn't work. At length she replies, "That's impossible. The one I turned into a pig was grown. Not a girl-thing like this one. Besides, I don't believe for a moment it escaped."

My arms slump to my sides, Em's train forgotten. My mouth is falling open and my belly goes sour. A pig turned up days after baby me arrived. She came right to our house and wouldn't leave the shed. When I could talk I called her—

"Find it, then." The king puts down the golden blade and faces Em. He is not smiling. "Produce the pig and turn it back into a mortal thing before all the court. At tonight's revel."

Em pulls in a hiss of breath. Then she smiles, big and false, and says, "Very well."

But there is no escape from the Otherworld. Granny said so. Acatica too. That's how the stories go. All of them.

"The walls will know if you leave the court." The king rubs his face with a huge rose petal, then lets it fall to the floor. "They'll be sure to whisper it to me."

"You don't trust me?" Em asks, and she's trying to sound prim and offended but really she sounds like she's hiding something. Like the king is right not to trust her.

"There's only one reason you'd go anywhere before the revel tonight. The walls will know to watch for it. If you leave, I'll know you for a liar. All the court will know it too."

Em is quivering with rage. She can't leave the kingdom under the mountain now. Which means she had every intention of doing so. Whoever she needs to find and turn back into a person isn't down here. That someone is a grown-up. Old enough to be a ma.

"One more thing." The king waves a hand across the pool of water hanging on the wall. It spirals smaller and smaller and disappears. "Tonight you will walk into the feast in the ninety-and-ninth row."

"*What?* You—"

"I do not recall giving you permission to use one of these things as your personal servant. You thought to win the privilege by finishing the job you started under the guise of tormenting the mortal girl for the amusement of the court, and you failed. Now here is one holding up your train, and you thought your dismal glamour could hide it? Did you honestly believe I'd look past the likes of you *defying* me?" The king shoulders past Em toward the door. On his way out, he gestures around the crystal room and says, "Clean."

Em buzzes something low and desperate. As she darts after him, her mist-train jerks out of my hands and shreds on the floor. The king said *clean* and there's no one here save me, but I'm not sure I can move.

The tattery woman who brought me to Woolpit turned up speaking gibberish and wearing green. She disappeared after handing me over, and no one ever found her body. Because she didn't disappear. She came back as Mother. The same servant Em turned into a pig for the sport of it.

Who somehow escaped the kingdom under the mountain.

Voices echo in the hallway, the king mocking and Em protesting. I'd better at least seem to be cleaning if they return. But as I try to collect myself, the basin quivers and goes fuzzy, and then the crystal falls away in shards to reveal a man crouching where the washing stand was just a moment before. He's in his middle years, bony and summer-brown, and his forearms are scratched with dozens of scars. The basin teeters on his shoulders around thatchy dark hair, bearing down so heavy that he's struggling to keep it from crashing to the glittering floor. He lowers the curved gem in groans and jags, and at last he straightens, rubbing his shoulders and wincing. Then he starts cleaning the room slow, like an ox with a whole field to plow.

The king must have been talking to him when he said *clean*. This man who is otherwise kept for endless days as a washing stand.

I pull in a sharp breath, loud enough that he glances at me. His mouth falls open, and before I can work out whether I should be afraid or curious or pitying or plain gobsmacked, tears slide down his cheeks and catch in his beard. "This can't be real," he croaks. "Lemme look at you. Closer."

I back up. I don't know what kind of grown-up he is. He steps nearer, half cringing, trying to smile, and that's when I fling myself at the door and almost crash into Em. A butterfly drifts out of her hair and a narrow plait sags. Her eyes are red like she's been crying, but her lovely, terrible face is steely.

"You," she says to the man. "You'll know. Where is she?"

He studies his feet and doesn't reply.

"The woman-thing," Em goes on, sharp and impatient. "Call to her. Make her come back. I know you were cozy with her. She'll come if you call her."

At that, he looks up. His eyes are brown, deep and rich like earth that wants a seed. He lifts his shoulders slow and sad, still crying, not bothering to hide it, and part of me wants to say something comforting because no one else here will do it.

Em wrinkles her nose in disgust and waves him back to his work like she's done so a thousand times. She stands, arms folded, watching his every limp and stoop and swipe. When the cleaning is done, he glances at me one more time, then kneels and shuffles the wash-basin back onto his shoulders. There's a whisper of that leaf-rot smell, and crystal climbs up his legs and midsection. His body goes smooth and slender and disappears entirely till he's a washing stand again, delicate and shiny.

I'm trying hard to breathe. *They can make nothing of their own.* The tables in that workroom, the chairs and settees, the king's throne—they're all mortal servants. Every last thing beneath the mountain once lived and breathed, and now must hold water or platters or the backside of one of Those Good People.

The walls were people once too. Acatica said so. Men and women who thought to escape. That must be why they hate the rest of us so much.

The pig bite on my leg is throbbing. It's still red and raw. Mother nipped me that first day the green children arrived at our house. At the time I was shocked; she's never so much as growled at me, even when I was small and pulled her ears and tail. But that bite only hurts when Those Good People are trying to make something *seem*. Mother took one look at the green children and knew exactly who they were, what they'd come for. She did the only thing she could to help me.

I always wondered why my first ma would leave me like she did. My Woolpit ma said mothers are always with their children, even when they can't be. It sounded like one of those kind things to say to a foundling, to make up for what they don't have because of other people's choices.

I never reckoned how there might be truth in it.

I dreamed of them again.

The king warned me this would happen when I walked once more the place where I grew up. Where I should have grown up, had the foreigners not come in their red tunics with long, curved shields and big swords. When they marched you could hear them, even far away, because their feet would hit the ground in unison, tromp tromp tromp, like they were one creature with one single will.

You will never be free of them, said the king. Enough of you bled out that the very ground remembers.

They came burning settlements. That's what we heard, and there was nothing for it but to fight or run, and given the ragged, haunted souls that sought refuge among us, it was more than clear that fighting would gain us very little. But there was nowhere to run. No way to keep ourselves if we did. The smoke rose from all directions. They'd be upon us soon. They were not like us. What they might want, only the gods knew, and our mothers had no wish for us to find out.

So the men and boys armed themselves. They formed up behind our chieftain and off they went to fight. My father went, and my brother, and both fell somewhere far away, along with enough of their fellows that there were not enough of ours left alive to bear their bodies home. They had to be left for the enemy, to do with what they would.

The last time I saw my mother, we'd fled as far as the stream. She hoped the foreigners would find goods enough to plunder in the houses and keep moving. A while back, she'd buried coins and jewelry near the holy well on the other side of the meadow and we would need to buy safety, wherever we tried to go. I was to wait at the edge of the greenwood where there'd be easy hiding if anyone should happen by, but she swore she'd be back before the sun was overhead. We would make our way north. My great-grandmother had married an Iceni blacksmith. Someone might still remember her.

I waited three days.

By sundown on that first day, I knew she wasn't coming. There was too much stillness, like I was the only living creature in a month's walk. I stayed the other two days because leaving made it real. Leaving meant I was well and truly on my own.

Leaving meant I might come across her body, wherever it lay lifeless. Whatever the foreigners had done to it.

There was nowhere to go. Nowhere to be where the world didn't smell like char. Serve me and live, *said the* king under the mountain, and I knew him from my grand-mother's stories but still I went with him through the green-wood and into the wolf pit ankle-deep with bones.

There are bones because there is sacrifice, *said the king, and as I followed, the walls began to whisper, telling me where my mother lay slain, my father and my brother, where their white bones lay bleaching.*

The walls are very interested in bones.

Mostly when I dream of the foreigners, I dream of the smoke and the tromp tromp tromp *of their tread. It's enough to wake me gasping, but when I wake, I am Agnes. Her dark is ordinary, the light a warm orange glow from the last of the fire. Now when I cry, it's for how commonplace everything is, how simple and comfort-ing. How there's a ma who'll put a hand on my back and murmur that all will be well. Like my first ma did when we crouched behind that stand of brush by the stream, her wispy hair tickling my cheek as she tried to keep the rasp of tears from her voice.*

Now when I wake, I am home again. Like those soldiers never came.

You want to find your little friend, don't you? whisper the walls. *Go ahead and try. Run through the corridors. We're hungry.*

I back slowly out of the crystal room and into the eerie greenlit corridor. Em is long gone, buzzing in a rage out of sight. A mouse hole appears in the wall across from me like a slow, creeping spill.

"Agnes?" Acatica's voice echoes through the hole. "Can you hear me? The cleaning work in the great hall is finished. We must lay the new table for tonight's revel."

I crouch and wrap my hands over my head. I should do as I'm told, but my legs are mush. Mother the pig used to be a servant under the mountain. Mother the pig is my first ma. Somehow she escaped and became a woman long enough to have me and make sure I'd be cared for.

I'll never see her again. I'll never see her as she really is—both my Mother and my ma.

My feet are made of rocks, same as the ground. Em smacked me with enough glamour that I'm not even myself anymore.

I stand up. However I seem, I am still Agnes Walter. If my first ma could get free of the Otherworld and stay with me, there must be a way I can get back to her. There must be a way I never have to return here.

The mouse hole grows larger as I approach it. Or mayhap I shrink. I'm able to move through it, though, and Acatica is waiting for me in yet another greenish corridor. Her arms are full of woven platters and she nods me into motion, chattering anxiously about how much there is to do.

I keep pace at her elbow, hurrying. "I know you said there was no escape, but my ma got out. She was turned into a pig and—"

"There is no escape," Acatica cuts in, and she sounds less angry than weary. She plows a pace ahead of me and into a workroom much like the one we were in not long ago. It's filled with kids with busy hands, weaving plates and mugs and cutlery.

"What happened to all the platters and things we made before?" I wiggle my fingers that were stumps and hide them in my skirt.

Acatica pulls a handful of dead leaves out of her apron and scatters them at my feet.

I take that in. The enormity of it. The *eternity* of it.

Every night these things will have to be made. Thousands upon thousands. They will fall apart by day, and we will have to remake them or be ourselves remade as washing stands or chairs or privy seats.

"But my ma's not here! The king all but said as much. She must—"

"No more of that," Acatica whispers, piling my arms with leaf-woven dishes and mugs. "It's trickery, whatever you think you heard. Our masters might not lie, but you still cannot believe anything they say. If your ma's not here, you don't want to know what's become of her. And say nothing more of escape where the walls can hear!"

Acatica hurries in front of me and I make myself follow. That business with the pig didn't sound like trickery, but she's been here long enough to see things I might not.

There's no one I can ask. No way to know for sure.

We step into a massive chamber that's squint-bright and bigger than I thought any room could be. It's half the size of Woolpit at least, and gloriously lit like midday in July. Lining the walls are dozens of statues. Each one is made of fine sand and tinted with different shades of earth so they look like real, living people. They're wearing strange garments I've never seen, and each fold is sculpted so perfectly that I have to look and look again just to be sure they're not really alive.

"Here." Acatica is moving toward a table so long I can't see the end of it, covered in a single white cloth, with hundreds and hundreds of chairs pushed tidily beneath. All those people. What they must have done, to be made to kneel forever on all fours and have hot food put on their backs.

Acatica begins laying leaf-woven dishes on the table, and the moment each one touches the cloth, it becomes the purest shining silver. I follow her lead, placing one platter before every chair. There are still mugs and cutlery to do and I try to keep up, but my hands are shaking.

There is someone I can ask. Someone without much more to lose. The man who's a washing stand. *She'll come if you call to her.* Mayhap he knows how she escaped. How she's managed to stay in Woolpit all these years without being snatched back. There must be a story. Only I wouldn't know how to get back to the crystal room if I tried, and I dare not try. Already the walls are watching me. I've said too much they don't like, and now they're waiting for a chance to drag me in and stuff my mouth with dirt and pin me down with the weight of stone.

When we get to the end of the table, the bottoms of my feet are worn blistery and the platters we place become gold instead of silver. This must be where the king sits, and the Crown Prince, and other noble lords and ladies. The walls are the palest green and the twigs that make the pictures are the thinnest wisps of wood. Acatica sighs, then starts the long walk back to the other end and the rest of the tableware.

I'm trying to stay angry at Senna. I'm trying not to *admire* Senna for being clever enough to get free of all this. Make the platters. Weave the glowworm dress. Serve the food. Stay very still and keep your head down, because there are worse things than fetching and carrying. Night after night after endless, timeless night.

The pig bite on my leg begins to ache, which makes me think of Mother and how she'd lay next to me when I was sitting alone splitting daisy stems with my thumbnail and feeling left out. How she'd listen, breathing steadily, when I told her my secrets and worries and fears. How hard it must have been to hand baby me over to a stranger and hope to whatever saints she knew that I'd be looked after.

My knees go out and I fold down near the wall. Close my eyes. I can't cry. My feet are throbbing. If I was the girl in the story, I'd know what to do. It would come easy, like things do for girls like Glory who are never at the edges of anything.

So mayhap I'm not the girl in this story after all. I don't know anything.

"I want to be," I whisper. "I want to be the girl in the story."

Will you tell us the story? the wall asks in a shy, hushed voice.

I leap back. It's a trick. It has to be.

Please don't go. The voice is small and hesitant. Like a timid child hoping to join the group. *We cried too much. We all got put here. Away from our mas. They're in other walls. We can't cry if we're near the king. He doesn't like it.*

"You all?" I repeat. "You're . . . children?"

At the far end of the hall, Acatica is making her slow way up the table, placing sticks bound with hedgeweed near every plate. Each bundle turns into a dainty silver goblet as it touches the cloth. I can't make her do all the work alone, but I can't force myself to move.

In front of me is something that's both a wall and children. It's neither one of these things nor the other.

If you don't tell us a story, we'll pull you in here with us, the wall says, and there's an edge of threat in its baby voice, eerie and sweet. *Then you can tell us stories forever.*

This is the kind of sticky trap that Those Good People love most, when you don't know whether doing a thing will end in a reward or a punishment. But the wall wants a story, and I have more stories than I know what to do with. Besides, doing a kind thing is still a kind thing, whether you're rewarded or punished.

I lean close to the pale, delicate twigs. I close my eyes, and I whisper the first story that comes to mind— my own. How I got here. The last story I might ever have to tell. Martin's sudden, terrible illness. Waking up in the pit. Senna's treachery. It's not whispering into flowers and shouting into rocks, but someone is hearing it. Someone will know what's become of me, even if it's a wall of half-mad children trapped in a prison of dirt and bones.

My hands sting. They're clasped tight in front of me like I'm hugging everyone I'll never see again. My parents. Glory. Mother the pig, who I would give anything to kneel beside and whisper *thank you* one hundred times into her silky ear.

When I open my eyes, I'm not in the feasting hall anymore. I'm alone in the corridor outside the crystal room where Em confronted the king. The wall behind me is wavering and fuzzy, shifting the smallest bit like baby Hugh curling up for sleep after I'd told him a bedtime story.

This wall is entirely children, and no kid can resist a bedtime story.

The crystal room stands empty, perfectly clean. Just as I pictured it in the moments before the wall spoke to me and I lulled it to sleep. I doubt I'll get another chance, so I tiptoe to the washing stand, kneel, and whisper, "Hello? Are you in there?"

"Is it you? Forgive me if I scared you. I just wanted a look." The voice is urgent and scratchy, like it's coming from deep in a pit. It's a man's voice, but the washing stand stays a glimmering pedestal balancing a basin on its slender neck. "I didn't want to hope. Nothing's worse than hope. But it's you. You look just like her."

I can see my likeness reflected in the smooth panes of crystal, and it's unsettling enough that I shift a little so I'm all in pieces.

"I'm called Agnes. I was here . . . earlier." Keeping track of time under the mountain is like swimming in fast water. At least I can use the revels to count the days.

"When your ma told me she was expecting you, I wept. You'd be born here. You'd never see a sky." The washing stand's voice cracks. "But I've lost so much. Gaining a little baby meant everything."

I had a first da, and even though the Woolpit mas had their own stories about him, in mine he was always a handsome lord somewhere, or a busy merchant who thought a baby would be happier living in a village than on some dusty road. Now I squint, trying to remember those few moments I saw him cleaning. The color of his hair. The wonder on his face. Slowly I say, "You're my da?"

"I am," the washing stand replies quietly. "Not that I'm much of one. I couldn't protect your ma. Or you."

"Is it true?" I glance at the walls, then lower my voice and speak right into the pedestal. "Did one of Those Good People turn my ma into a pig?"

"She was humiliated. She kept saying how no one could love her like that. I didn't care. Nothing could make me love her any less. I told her again and again. That she was beautiful. That us being together made this place bearable. But she started saying how she knew a way she could leave and stay gone. How she couldn't bear the thought of you being born a piglet here."

"Only birth and death can stop the seeming," I whisper, and for once the Woolpit mas were right. There *was* something unusual about the tattery woman who'd staggered into the village and given me up. Leaving the kingdom under the mountain meant she'd have no chance to be human again. Those Good People would never take the seeming off her. After having me, the seeming would come back and she'd stay a pig for good. And she did it for me. Giving up something for someone else is the purest form of love.

Little wonder sacrifice is one of the few things that forces the Otherworld to stop and take heed.

The washing stand sighs. "I begged her not to. She was all I had left, and she had you in her belly. A baby or a piglet, I didn't care. Either way you'd be mine. But she . . . well. Soon enough, no one could find her. Our masters demanded I tell them what I knew. They didn't believe me when I said I knew nothing. They *did* believe when I told them that even if I knew, they wouldn't get it out of me. Mostly they couldn't have me spreading it around that one of us *things* got out. So here I am."

"Here you are," I echo sadly.

"I don't know which would be worse," the washing stand whispers. "For her to be down here still, keeping away from me because she's ashamed, or for her to have made it out of the Otherworld only to have you snatched back and trapped here like the rest of us."

"She's well. But she's still a pig."

"I don't care." The washing stand's voice is low and raw. "She's alive. That's all that matters. I love her no matter what."

"Me too," I whisper.

We sit there together in the glittering quiet of the crystal room. I lean my head against the pedestal and it makes a small sound, like a muffled sob.

"Da?" I bite my lip. "You said my ma knew a way to get out. She was a pig while I was in her belly, so mayhap I can use that same way. Did she tell you what it was?"

"You're going to leave?" the washing stand asks plaintively. "But I just met you."

"If you're really my da, wouldn't you want me to be free of this terrible place?"

"I should. I do. Just . . . you're all that's left of her. Of anyone I've ever loved. How can I want anything but for us to be together?"

My throat is closing. There's no leaf-rot smell. Nothing of glamour. I watched him weep outright. This isn't a trick, and my whole insides hurt.

"The others have forgotten me," the washing stand

says. "I have no kin. No one I knew from before, when the soldiers came. I'm all alone here now."

"I could bring you with me. Somehow. I won't leave you alone."

The washing stand is quiet for a long, long moment. At last it whispers, "Yes, you will. But I'll tell you anyway."

"I won't! I—"

"She said the wind drifted in sparkling whispers along the hallways," the washing stand cuts in. "There's but one way wind could get under the mountain, and that's through a door that leads outside of it. Pigs can see the wind, you know. They're the only animals that can."

It's so pretty, too. Little silvery currents that whirl and glide like weeds in a stream. It was never a story. There's some piglet part of me that can see the wind.

"The walls must have overlooked her. They listen especially for whispering and secrets, and she likely marched right past them as if she had nothing to hide. With glamour still on her, she must have found her way to the crossing place and made it through."

The washing stand is crying now, softly, like it can't go on. This is a place where things only seem, so I slide closer and put both arms around the slender crystal pedestal. Its edges dig into my shoulder and hip, but I cling tight and hug hard. "It's all right. Don't cry. You won't be alone."

"Well, well. This is unusual."

I whip around, and there in the doorway is the king under the mountain. Every bit of me wants to scrabble away, but I'm frozen and it's not because of glamour.

"Ah . . ." I cast around for the first thing that makes sense. "She sent me. The one who had an audience. It wasn't my idea. She told me to come here. To . . . ah . . ."

The king waits till the words slip and dart and wing away from me. Then he says, "The walls heard you whispering in this place all alone. So I heard you as well."

"She lost a hair pin," I finally manage, "and she told me to look for it. But it's not here."

"Not under the washing stand," the king replies, almost a taunt, almost a question.

"No. Sire." I climb to my feet. It gives me time to put words together. He found me where I shouldn't be, and words are all I have now. "Sire, why am I here? I've done you no wrong."

"We care nothing for right and wrong. We take what we're owed, and what we're owed is blood. This is a question of sacrifice."

A life for a life, traded by whatever means.

"I—I thought it was a bargain."

The king hitches a shoulder. "In this case, it's both."

"I mean no insult," I say, careful, careful, "but how do you know my blood belongs to you?"

"The mortal girl called out from the crossing place in

her own tongue," the king replies. "No one could hear her unless they shared the blood."

Senna said the same thing, and nobody else in Woolpit so much as lifted their heads from their work. At least one thing she told me was in truth.

"But her people are Trinovantes," I say, "and there are none in Woolpit."

"She is from where you are from," the king replies, "but she is not from *when* you are from."

I frown. Woolpit has always simply *been*. Then again, Granny was once my age, and she had her own granny, who also had a granny. One of them must have been listening to the rocks and flowers and heard Acatica and the others calling and whispering, hoping someone would hear.

"It's not right." I lift my chin. So far boldness cut with courtesy has served me well, and the king has yet to realize I'm a piglet he has overlooked. "My grandmother always said your people were fair. She said you might not always be as kind as you could be, but you never lied and you never promised something and then didn't give it."

The king narrows his eyes. "I gave them *exactly* what I promised. And as for kind? I did them a kindness they didn't deserve. All those pathetic farmers and their hoes and shovels, facing down the legions of Rome. The Trinovantes. The Iceni. The rest. They *begged* me to save them. Me and their gods. Their gods did not save them. *I* did."

"A kindness? Then why did Senna want so badly to leave?"

The king's dark look falters and he almost smiles. "You are more clever than you look."

I don't reply. Being clever under the mountain seems like a good way to get yourself turned into a rat. Those Good People cannot be stopped, challenged, or defeated, but they can be outwitted and tricked by anyone with wit enough to carry it off.

Those Good People reward clever even as they despise it.

"Perhaps this is what you're looking for?" The king holds out a finger, and on it perches a butterfly that's slowly closing its delicate orange wings.

He knows I gave a false reason for being here. I know it too. Still I croak, "Yes. Thank you. Sire."

"You should take it to her right away." The king snaps his fingers and a rat appears in the doorway of the crystal room. I offer one shaking hand and the butterfly obediently drifts onto it. It could be a leaf. It could be a girl like me who misses home.

It could be a girl like me who was careless with her whispering.

My first da has kept my ma a secret for this long, but after tonight, when Em will have to produce the pig or admit she let it escape, there will be no more secret. One way or another, I cannot be here when that happens. It won't be long before they work out how Mother got free, and I'll be trapped here for good.

I cannot rest easy till All Hallow's Eve has come and gone. I tack the iron needles to our door crosswise and stay up all night stiff on my pallet, listening to the fairy wretches clatter past on this, one of their high holy days when they ride and riot. Ma and Da sleep soundly but I hear every hoof-fall. I feel every cold whisper through the thatch.

But the morning after, I wake up in my bed. Ma hands me some porridge and kisses my forehead like it's any other day, and I smile so big and grateful that Da asks me all teasing if I have a sweetheart.

I'm safe. I'm well and truly free.

Kate is tall and bony, with a great torrent of red hair that barely stays beneath her hood. Tabby's front teeth were knocked out long ago by a stray hoof while she was milking, and she talks in whistles. They are glamoured easy. They are used to believing things they wish were true, and I hardly have to brush the fairy cloth before they are Agnes's dearest forever friends.

I arrange for us to wash clothes together one bright day just into the blood moon time, and I invite Glory to join us. She is desperate to have these girls as friends, and if I bring us all together in a tight little flock, I'll win her over for sure.

Only Glory takes one look at me, smiling there with Kate and Tabby standing as close to me as bark on an oak, and her eyes narrow. She makes some excuse and hurries away, and when I catch up with her, she hisses, "There's no need to show me up, Green Agnes. I'll not have someone be my friend out of pity."

The next day, the reeve starts watching me.

He wanders near a house where I'm helping the wife dye skeins of wool with a bitter brew of walnut shells, and he happens past when I'm minding a tiny toddling child while her mother takes a much-needed rest. Other times I spot him speaking in mutters to some of the men as they thresh or fix things, and they shrug and make the friendly, unhelpful gestures I direct them toward. Once the reeve appears near the mill where I'm looking for that bad pig who doesn't like me, and he raises an eyebrow when I tell him she's reluctant to sleep in her byre.

Chore by chore, errand by errand, Agnes has been making herself the darling of Woolpit, but the reeve constantly idling nearby makes people smile and wave me along. They don't want my help if someone is there to notice, and I must use the fairy cloth to change their minds again and again.

One rainy afternoon, the reeve turns up at our house. *Glory is with him, bundled in a nubby brown cloak that's trailing salt from every hem. It is so clearly her ma's doing that it's hard to be angry. Her ma is trying to protect her. It's what mas do. Even so, that much salt is going to muddle my glamour, and I cannot have it.*

"May I take your cloak?" *I smile at Glory, open and pleasant, all the while cursing myself. I should have directed Kate and Tabby to befriend Glory, not me. I should have seen how it would look—me taking something from her instead of inviting her into it.*

"I'll keep it," *she replies, and even though she smiles back, she is not the girl Agnes would have as a friend, but Glory Miller from the pit.*

Ma dips them each a mug of ale and shows them to the bench, but they do not sit.

"It's come to my attention that the green girl has learned our tongue," *the reeve says, and I pull in a sharp, silent breath because it was not supposed to come to anyone's attention. It was simply supposed to be, like it was never any other way.*

"You should have said something," *the reeve tells* Ma. "Sir Richard would very much like to know how she and the boy found themselves here and where they came from. He won't like knowing this was kept from him."

"What does it matter where they came from?" *Ma asks*

with just the smallest bit of an edge. "She's happy here. They both are."

"Surely you want these children to be reunited with their parents." The reeve peers at her. "Do you not?"

Ma takes long moments to reply. As far as she's concerned, Martin is playing somewhere nearby, or staying at a friend's hearth overnight. She has not asked about the old Agnes since All Hallow's Eve.

I will not take chances, though, not with this, so I rub the scrap of fairy cloth in my apron and Ma says, "Their parents may be dead. Or gone. These two are like my own children now."

"Your own," the reeve repeats, and I smile. But Glory elbows him, salt spilling from her hem, and the reeve startles visibly and goes on. "Sir Richard feels he has asked too much of you and your husband, keeping them all this time. With winter coming on and all. He insists that they're most welcome at the manor house."

After everything it took to get here, out from under anyone's thumb—no, I will not have it. But the reeve is speaking slow and reluctant. He did not like how his chieftain thought to keep lost children from their ma and da. If it were left to him, the reeve would look for my parents till his eyes bled, even though they have not walked this place for a thousand years.

He needs an excuse to keep looking. Something he can take back to his chieftain, but I can give him nothing that will do him much good or he will quickly see it for the falsehood it is. So I say, "I don't know how we got here. We were following our father's cattle, then we heard a sound. Then we found ourselves in the pit."

There. It'll take him a while to speak to everyone within ten days' walk who has more than one cow to follow.

Glory cocks her head. "Sound? What sound?"

"It was . . ." I cast about for words. I did not plan on Glory turning up with her hem full of salt. "The ringing. That we hear sometimes in the day."

"You mean the bells?" She frowns. "From the abbey of Saint Edmund? Surely you come from a place where you'd know the sound of bells. Bells that are rung in churches."

I am rubbing the fairy cloth hard now. Every god wants a sacrifice. The gods brought by the soldiers were no different.

"Father says she will not go to mass." The reeve speaks polite and careful still, but honed, and he keeps glancing at Ma and that's when it hits me. He's not as sure anymore that I'm a lost child, and he's trying to protect her and Da, too, just in case. He's trying to protect them from me.

Mayhap his hem is full of salt as well. Glory's ma wants me nowhere near her family.

Ma puts her arm across my shoulders and pulls me close. "Agnes goes to mass. What a terrible thing to say."

The reeve starts three different times to speak. Finally

he manages, "Mistress, I won't call you a liar in your own house."

"Ask your daughter." Ma is on her feet now, indignant. "Agnes stands with Glory often, and those other girls, too. The redhead and the one who lisps."

I run one bare toe across the hard-packed dirt floor. One day I will go to mass. It's what Agnes does, and I am Agnes now. Today I rub the fairy cloth and the reeve blinks and suddenly remembers that of course Agnes goes to mass. But I study the floor as I do it. I cannot command Woolpit with glamour forever. Not if I simply want to be Agnes.

"Speaking of Agnes." The reeve clears his throat. "Where is she?"

"Right here." Ma takes my hand and smiles down at me, and my insides go melty like a warm summer shower.

"Agnes," the reeve replies, "with the fair hair. Your daughter."

"Her?" Ma shrugs irritably. "Who cares about—"

"You've seen Fair Agnes," I tell him. "She left for the well not long ago. You must have seen her on the path."

"I must have seen her on the path."

"I remember a river, where we came from." I speak clear and gentle. The reeve cannot leave here thinking something's amiss with the old Agnes. He has to leave here on a hunt for rooster eggs. "A broad, rushing river. All the land around was green. So beautiful and full of growing things."

My first da would make fish traps out of willow wands and we'd weight them with stones and set them in that river. He'd bring some bread and we'd eat it on our walk home, through endless meadows, toward our fields and garden that all but sang with growing. Not even a thousand-thousand years could change this place so much. If it'll take the reeve seasons to speak with everyone with more than one cow, walking every patch of green in this place, every stretch of river, will take him years.

Years I will happily spend here.

"Green." The reeve nods as if he's putting it to memory. "There was a river."

I show him and Glory to the door. "Look for our parents if you must, but I'm happy here. This is my home now."

Later today I'll offer to help the housewives collect bark for tanning. I'll thresh and winnow on the morrow, and wind yarn and even tread flax. Chore by chore, errand by errand, Woolpit is coming around and I am leading it by the nose. The reeve may have the ear of the chieftain in the grand house, but the mas will put him firmly in his place if he thinks to raise an eyebrow at me. The fewer questions about the boy-thing and the old Agnes, the easier it will be for people to forget they were ever here.

Ma tugs me back to the fire and sits me down on the best part of the bench. "You never have to leave if you don't want to. You know that, right? You are our baby, like you were born to us."

It warms me all the way through. "Want me to get more wood for the fire?"

"Definitely not." Ma groans to her feet. "You need your rest."

That is not something a ma would say. Ever.

By spring I will be able to bury this piece of fairy cloth. All of Woolpit will believe me to be the girl I've always been. I'll do it. I will.

As soon as I know for sure that no one can ever make me leave.

I'm certain this rat is lost. Instead of taking me down elegant corridors made of lovely twig pictures toward Em's chamber, we're crawling down a dank-smelling hallway that's barely lit by guttering greenish lamps every stone's throw. When the rat stops next to a fraying linen curtain with a moldy hem, I actually ask it, "Where are we? This can't be right," as if it could answer.

Em claws back the curtain. Her wheat-pale hair is long and flyaway over both shoulders, and she's wearing a musty dressing gown. "What are you doing here?"

I dare not reply, so I hold up my hand where the orange butterfly still clings gamefully to my finger.

"That *brrzzzzzz*," she mutters, and I shiver because I know a swear when I hear one. She swipes the butterfly off my hand and crushes it in her fist. I squeak and flinch, but only fragments of a dry leaf scatter to the floor. "Taunt me, will he? I'd give much to see how *he'd* like it, being made the fool."

Em grabs my wrist and hauls me into the room, jerking the curtain closed. I stumble into a narrow wooden bed made up with a colorless blanket. There's not much else in the room because there's no space for it. A single chair with dead moss and rocks and tiny round bones piled on the seat. A peg on the wall, empty. There's a faint shine of greenish light from the ceiling that seems to leak from the cracks, and the leaf-rot smell is thick like summer sweat.

Em sees me glancing around and says, "Dreadful, isn't it? It's taking all my will just to make it decent. My other chamber is gone. Like it never was. All my gowns, my bed, my shoes—everything. My punishment, the king says. Till I produce that dratted pig."

It just seems, I want to tell her. But whether it's real doesn't matter here. Whatever glamour she has must pale against the king's.

"So not only must I walk into the revel in the ninety-and-ninth row," Em goes on, "but I must do it as I stand. Barefoot, and practically in rags."

I stay near the door. My feet are made of the same coarse rubble as the ground. My hands the same linen as the curtain.

"The way I see it," Em says calmly, "it's your fault I'm here. In this hole in the wall. In the ninety-and-ninth row."

She says it like Glory would. Simple and straightforward, like there's no split to work in a chisel and gain a handhold. No way for me to say, *But all I did was stand there. You were the one who needled the king. You were the one who overstepped her bounds, and not by accident, either. You were the one who turned my ma into a pig just for the fun of it and she got away and now you're in trouble.*

I open my mouth to beg her pardon. Like I would if she were Glory. But it's *not* my fault Em was punished. Just like it's not my fault that the May King was cruel to Glory. It would have cost him nothing to dance with her just once.

Em wants something. She's not content with what she has. I may not be one of Those Good People, but I know what it is to want something so much you'll give almost anything to get it. I know what it is to feel it's so close that all you must do is give up one more thing.

I know what it is to want someone to simply listen and *believe.*

"The way I see it," I say, "it's the king's fault you're here."

She swivels to face me, squinting like she's trying to decide whether to turn me into a rat or hear me out.

"The king means to embarrass you," I go on, and I wish Glory were here so she could hear it too, "but if you turn up at the revel anyway, who looks the fool then? Not you. You're the one who can hold her head up no matter when she walks in. No matter what she's wearing."

"There's still the pig. If I don't turn it back into the mortal thing it was before all the court, I will never hear the end of it. Worse than that, I'll stay in this hole in the wall forever. No more gowns. No more carpets." Em grabs my chin and peers into my face. "The king is wrong. You cannot be that pig. Yet somehow you must be the pig."

Those Good People rarely have babies of their own so she's not thinking along those lines, but if she sits too long with it, she will work it out. Em wants things, and I must make it feel possible that she will have them. So I say, "At least let me make you a dress to wear. Then I should go back. Before the king notices I'm gone and you get in trouble again."

"What's it to you?"

The girl in the story knows Those Good People will always listen to flattery. "Whoever's fault it is that you're here, I don't want to be on your bad side."

Em fidgets with threads loosening from her cuff. "Very well. It *is* your fault, after all."

I kneel beside the chair and pick through the rubbish on the seat. There's moss, sure enough, and sticks and leaves, but also a handful of tiny bones the size of my smallest fingernail. Bones make me think of meat, which makes the whole room smell like the tastiest supper the manor house could offer, which makes my belly light up with stings and jabs of hunger, but I fight it and keep working. The bones are a bit like glowworms, only not easily biddable like things that are alive. They must be coerced. Slick tendons appear and slither around the bone ends to join them, just like something living. A tiny headache sprouts in the middle of my forehead, but I keep weaving till the bones run out.

"What do you think?" I hold up what I've made so far. A bodice, laced together with the tenderest wisps of sinew.

Em brushes admiring fingers against it and the bones whisper *clickety-tick*. "Oh yes. Keep going."

"I used all the bones. Can you get more?"

She bangs her fist twice on the wall and a heap of bones grows at my feet. They're stripped bare and smooth to the touch, like they've been bleaching at the bottom of a pit.

A life for a life, by whatever means. There are bones because there is sacrifice.

Em is sitting on the edge of the narrow bed toying with her hair, pulling it up this way and braiding it that way. She is already halfway to the revel and paying me no mind. With slow, quiet motions, I start slipping the smallest bones under my folded skirts. One by one. A handful. Soon, the only bones left in the towering pile are bulky and thick. Thigh bones and ribs, half a skull.

"Beg pardon, but these are too big," I say. "The dress will look silly. I need little ones."

Em frowns at the pile and kicks it a few times. Then she sighs and raps on the wall again. Another gush of bones rises in the pile, and when she goes back to fiddling with her hair, I hide the tiny ones till none are left. When I ask a third time, Em hits the wall so hard that bones fill half the room in a heap taller than my head.

I hide small bones steadily. There's a mound of them now and they dig into my bare legs under my skirt. It's all I can do not to squirm.

"I'm sorry." I hold up a pair of huge collarbones. "I suppose I'll have to use these big ones. I'm sure your gown won't look *too* ridiculous."

"Numbwit good-for-nothing walls," Em growls. "Think this is funny, do you? There are plenty of ways to get bones around here."

She buzzes angrily into the corridor, and when I leap up to make sure she's out of sight, the curtain won't budge. It's like a sheet of rock, unmoving and solid. I couldn't escape if I tried. But I don't mean to get out. Not now. Not yet. Em must go to the revel believing she has beaten the king at his own game.

I don't want to think about the ways there are to get bones around here. I have what I need. Before Em returns, I must make a pig.

First a cage of bones, then moss as muscle and skin. My hands are still littered with cuts atop cuts from the wheat field, not a one of them healed, and my blood slicks over the monstrous thing in drips and smears. I close my eyes and think of Mother, her bristly skin and sturdy trotters and loppy, folded-over ears. She got me out of here once. With any luck she can do it again with this blood we share that must serve.

Glamour makes things seem, but surely there are limits. Making yard waste and bones seem like a living thing might be one of them. It doesn't have to seem for that long, though. Just until the king calls Em to account.

When I open my eyes, a pig-thing stands before me. It wavers on legs that are too skinny, and its eyes are flat and blank like the rocks they truly are. But Em will want to see a pig, so she will see one.

Bones cover half the small room knee-deep. I heap them near the door so the pile is almost to my waist, then carve out a hole and tuck the pig-thing inside. The poor creature makes no sound and sways on its little trotters. I cover the hole carefully and arrange more bones over it so nothing of the hole or the pig is visible.

Then I whisper a prayer to any saint listening, pour the mound of little bones I hid back into the pile, and pick up making the dress like nothing is amiss. I'm working the last part of the skirt when Em sweeps in, the curtain dancing like ordinary linen once more. Without a word, she pours a basketful of tiny bones onto the floor by my knees. They rattle and bounce everywhere, like hail on hard-packed ground.

I wait till Em throws herself back onto her bed, then I ask, "Can I move the bigger bones into the corridor? There are so many. It'll go faster if I can find the small ones easier."

Em makes an impatient shooing gesture, and I set aside the bone dress and start shifting the pile. The curtain moves easily now. I move bones by the armload. Soon enough Em is bored again and braiding her hair, so I uncover the opening in the side of the pile and move the pig like it's any other load. I set it on its trotters in the corridor where it staggers like someone fed it barley mash from a brewing.

Most of the big bones are in the corridor. Hundreds of tiny ones spread over the floor like a carpet of fallen stars. I make one last trip into the hallway. The pig is where I left it, nose pointed at the floor, ears limp and listless. I pet its head, even though it's not real. Poor hapless thing.

Then I pinch its tail hard and dart back into the chamber. I'm kneeling in the bones when the pig bleats weakly, not even close to a squeal, and Em looks up.

"What was that?" she asks.

The walls listen to whispers and secrets especially, so I look up from my work as if I'm bewildered at her interruption.

Em rocks to her feet and looks under her bed, then behind the chair. My heart is racing, but I keep glamouring bones into the gown one after another. Once she finds that pig, I want her heading to the revel as soon as possible. I can't give her too much time to look it over and work out it's not what she thinks it is.

The curtain twitches. Em steps past me and pulls it back, then lets out a wordless screech of joy. She is buzzing again, high and triumphant, and shoves me hard out of her way so she can push the pig into the chamber. She doesn't know to look for the tail that curls over and not under, or the chipped front hoof. Everything that makes Mother who she is. I fight down a smile and force the last few tiny bones onto the hem of the long, clickety skirt.

Em holds the curtain aside and peers up and down the hallway. "Hey. Rats! You were promised a reward for finding this pig and you shall have one. Rats? Hmm. They must not like the bones." She lets the curtain fall and mutters, "It's about time something went right."

"Your gown is ready," I say, and when I hold up the dress of bones, Em's eyes go big with the closest thing to excitement I've seen from any of Those Good People. I rattle it so the whole thing goes *tickety-tick* and tempts her vanity because she absolutely cannot try to turn my pig-thing into my ma right now because in no way will it work. It can barely stand of its own power. She must put the gown on and leave so I can flee this place.

Only that means I'm leaving Acatica. I'm leaving my da.

If I don't leave, I may never see them again anyway.

I help Em dress as quick as I can, chattering all the while how no one else at the revel will have anything like it, and she spins to admire herself. The tiny bones chitter along her shoulders and shush around her feet.

"They will surely look at me when I enter," Em says, smug and haughty. "Even in the ninety-and-ninth row."

"You should go right now," I tell her. "Mayhap if you show the king you have the pig, he'll let you walk in earlier. He wouldn't want to keep the others from the spectacle he promised."

Em scoops up the pig in her arms. The poor thing looks instants from shattering into moss and knuckles and stones. I would struggle with a beast that size, but it lies in her arms like a sack of wet barley. Then she's gone without a backward glance, without so much as a word of thanks, and the curtain dances behind her.

I have made Em think she has everything she wants, but it won't be long before she realizes she's been tricked. It'll happen in front of the whole of the fairy court, too. She'll try to pull the glamour off the pig-thing, but instead of my ma, it'll be—

Laughing. Pointing. Like Glory last May Eve.

I can be nowhere near here when it happens.

Once Em is well and truly gone, I stand in front of the wall. There is no one who doesn't like a story, whether it's bedtime or not.

I lean close and start whispering.

Today I slipped out to fetch water. I'm shivering my way down the path in a rush because if Ma spots me, she'll whisk the bucket away and insist I go play. Find Glory and Kate and Tabby. Spend the day cozied up by the fire with my spinning.

The old Agnes was never allowed such leisure.

There is no rest under the mountain. The fair folk revel every night, wining and dancing, and time in that place ebbs and flows according to their whims or requirements. Nights can last a night, or they can last a month or a year or a thousand-thousand timeless ages. There is no end to their needs. No patience for resistance or tears or moping. Idle feet are turned into benches. Idle hands become tables. Those who simply will not obey are drawn into the walls where they can look upon freedom while going slowly mad. There is no warning. There is no pleading. Anyone who does not work is made useful in some other way.

So every night my hands carried. They got burned by hot plates and cut to bits by sharp leaves. Every night my feet scurried, usually away from a smack aimed at my head or under an armload of golden dishes streaked with gravy and heaped with bones that would turn back to leaves in an eyeblink.

I would not bow to them, though. They did not like it. They did not like how I found ways to stand next to others—not just Trinovantes, but Iceni and Cantiaci and even Catuvellauni—so we could keep ourselves alive in whispers.

My ma made the best roast.

My sweetheart's brother is wed to your cousin. That makes us kin.

My grandda inked these marks on my back.

Our feet began to slow. Our eyes strayed up from our work. We were forgetting how we swore to serve, how we agreed to become nothing but our hands and feet. We were forgetting how we had agreed to an eternity that was both a bargain and a sacrifice while also being neither, and we'd done it to save ourselves.

I thought we were beneath notice. I was wrong.

Her name in whatever tongue the fair folk speak was a muttery buzz in my ear, and all I could be sure of was the sound it began with. Emmmmmmsomethingbuzzy-mutterevilevilevil. The first time she summoned me, I thought I was done for. But instead she took my hand and

the wall rushed at me—dirt—rocks—bones—just as it did when I first came under the mountain. She'd taken me to the crossing place, and day after day I followed her into the harsh yellow light of the world beyond.

The first thing you'd see was the bodies. Where the soldiers came from, rebels were nailed alive to crossed pieces of wood and left there to die slowly, but there were too many rebels here for them to bother making crosses. Instead the bodies were impaled. A single sharpened post was driven into the ground with a man skewered on it, the bottom part through his nether regions and the top stabbing through his shoulder, or his chest, or his gaping, silent mouth. Sometimes a boy my age. One time, a girl with a tangle of hacked-off scarecrow hair, stripped to her shift and cut to pieces, and I was sick all over myself.

After the bodies, you'd see the houses. What was left of them, anyway. People were still living in them the first few times, but these were not the proud, cheerful men and women I remembered. They were thin and hooded, scurrying, their eyes always to the horizon. There was no one I remembered. There were soldiers, though. The men of Rome who did not think it enough to burn it down, but decided to make a home in the boneyard of it, as if no one had lived there before.

After a while, there were only stray dogs in the settlement, then heaps of earth began drifting over the houses and byres and sheds, like the ground itself thought to bury the dead that no one else would or could.

"No amount of whispering or memories will bring them back," the fairy girl would say. "The men of Rome have made this place a burying ground, and now they have gone. Like none of you were ever here."

It hurt too much to think about. So I fetched and carried. I stopped whispering to the others. Her work done, the fairy girl left me in peace and went back to her feasting and plotting. She could have just turned me into a stepstool, but there was no amusement for the fairy court in that. No reward from the king, either.

But I never forgot how my ma would run her fingers through my hair while she told me stories. I never forgot how my da taught me to carve an apple and weave a fishing basket. I never forgot what it was to go to sleep at night knowing they were near, that they would keep me safe.

If there were no more mas out there, no more das, no more girls to weave flower crowns and suppers to eat and long starlit nights to tell stories in, I'd gotten the better end of the bargain. Since under the mountain I would never age or wither or die, those things would live forever deep within me.

But something was amiss. On their high holy days, the fair folk would ride. Every May Eve, every All Hallow's Eve, they put on their finest garments and left us with a *mighty mess to clean, so many soiled plates and spills and rubbish everywhere that we'd barely have it done by the time they clattered back, all high spirits and boasting.*

If there were no mortals to sport with, to trick and torment and reward, the fair folk had no reason at all to leave their realm.

I poured strong red wine on the walls, and they got drunk and let me go where I liked. I went straight to the crossing place. Somehow it had become a pit, and there, crouched among the white bones of wolves and children, I hoped and I hoped hard. A hut. A shack. A tent, even. Just one living person who might meet my eye and nod.

I steeled myself, then climbed up halfway. Snuck a quick peek over the top in case there were worse things than ever the soldiers did to us.

Houses stood where none had been for ages. People everywhere—mas and das, grannies and granddas, house-wives and husbandmen, kids of all sizes. They looked nothing like me. They spoke a tongue I did not know. They were not Trinovantes and they were not Roman. They were something else entirely, but they cooked and plowed and bickered and hugged and herded and sang, the kids throwing dirt clods and giggling, tending lambs, pulling hair.

Making flower crowns.

It was foolhardy, going back, but I couldn't stay away. I drank in das carrying kids on their shoulders. Mas making cheese and butter. Kids splashing in the stream ford and girls picking apart the exact *way Aelfred looked at Eahlswith at the revel last month. I learned their tongue, my ears still full of glamour. I hung on the edge of the crossing place till my arms went numb. And after the fairy girl realized what I was doing and made it so I could never go back—not when the people above the mountain whispered and grew hostile, and especially not when the walls knew to look for me—instead of putting my head down and fetching and carrying and forgetting, I made a plan.*

"Goodness, Agnes, what are you doing out here? It's freezing, and you should be indoors." Ma steps out of the pig byre as I'm trying to sneak up the path. "You haven't been fetching water, have you? Here, give that over and go play."

"But Ma, I don't mind. Really."

"Nonsense!" Ma takes the bucket and wails when she sees my cold-reddened hands. "We must wrap those right now. You'll get frostbite!"

"Yes, Ma." It's easier than arguing. I shove my hands into my apron and run my fingers over the scrap of fairy cloth. Something's not right. Ma should be treating me like Agnes. Instead she's treating me like a baby.

Or mayhap it's working just as I mean it to. Ma is loving me hard and consuming, like a fire. She's loving me like something that must be protected at all costs. Not like she'd love a child who must make a mistake or two *and learn from them, who is strong and smart enough to do it.*

No. It's working like the boy-thing intended. Tempting me to use something beyond my control with the hopes of gaining things I'm not meant to have.

I pull the cloth from my apron. I must be done with it. Agnes did not have to glamour her ma and da for them to love her. I am Agnes and I must do the same.

Instead of going inside, I slip around the house and into the garden where I dig a hole and shove in the scrap of fairy cloth. Then I stand up, trembling, my foot primed near the pile of dirt, hesitating, hesitating, willing myself to fill in the hole.

She might stop loving me at all. She might turn away from me. I will have nowhere to go. I will lose another ma.

The cloth is back in my hand. Back in my apron. I'm shaking all over. I fill in the empty hole with one swift sweep of my foot.

This wall insists I'm telling the story wrong. It keeps interrupting and calling me bad names and threatening to pull me in, but soon enough it goes fuzzy with sleep and there's a dizzying clamor of voices and a *shush* of gritty brown wind as I pass through.

I blink, and I'm in a grand corridor, one of the kind that all look alike, lit faintly green and arching high and cold above my head. The walls on either side are faded, deep in dreams, so I move quick.

A single gust of silver turns along the floor. In Woolpit, I tried not to look for the wind. It was hard to stop watching once I started, and it would be pretty and fold on itself and glitter, and then I'd get a cuff to the ear and a grown-up shouting at me to *step lively*. But now I squint into the dim. I start thinking about Mother, and curls of wind drift like dust in a sunbeam, and corners appear in the hallways where none were before. Then more corridors and corners, more winks and glimmers, and I stop thinking much at all and just follow.

They lead me toward music.

It's muffled by distance, but there's a lute and a lyre spinning a brisk circle dance, and flutes and the clattering of spoons and laughter and the tromp of dancing feet. Gleeful shrieking and rumbling and the sound of small things breaking.

The revel. It has to be.

If I wasn't following the wind, I'd think I was being lured. I can't turn back, though. Not given what'll happen with Em and the pig-thing, especially considering how much the king may already know thanks to those dratted walls. I must escape or face eternity as a rat—or worse.

The noise gets louder as I slink near, and soon enough, I turn into a corridor where open doorways spill blocks of firelight every twenty paces into the green-glow dim. At the end of the hallway is a staircase, and whispering all the way up are silvery glints of wind. I'll have to move past these three doorways without any of Those Good People seeing me.

I lift my hands. They're mostly skin again, but there's a pattern pressed deep into them. Wall-twigs if I hold them up, floor stones if I move them down. Whatever that glamour-dust was that Em blew on me—when?—must be wearing off. Music fills the chamber and the hallway, too, and the laughter and talk all but drown it out, so I don't have to try for tiptoe-quiet. At the first doorway I cautiously peek inside.

I mean only to be sure no one's looking at the door, but I stare outright at the sprawling room lit by thousands of tiny blazes of firelight. It's as big as the feasting hall where Acatica and I laid the table not long ago, and Those Good People are drifting here and there, gathering in twos and threes to smoke and chatter, pressed against the wall and kissing in a way that makes my face go hot. The rotty glamour smell is thick and my pig bite hurts in a steady hum; a lot of seeming must be going on here. No one's paying this doorway any mind and I'm about to dart past it, when someone catches my eye.

It's Acatica. She's across the hall between two of those sculptures that look like people made of sand, and she's holding a dish of sliced honey. *Don't leave me. Take me with you. I'm begging.*

Her plea glides into my head clear and direct, and I pull back into the hallway out of sight. I can save her. No more rats and vicious walls. No more bloody stumps for fingers. I'll move slow. Those Good People won't notice me. They're too busy reveling to pay heed to one mortal thing.

The pig bite on my leg throbs.

I peek again. *Please. You have to.* Acatica's whole face is frantic. Her hands like claws around the dish she's holding. I can't leave her here. Not like this. Or my da. They may have made a bargain, but it was a bad bargain. No one makes good decisions when they're scared.

My foot moves forward on its own. Toward the doorway. It's not every day I have a chance to help someone. To *save* someone. I'll take her hand and we'll slip down this hallway and up those stairs and—

I stumble. My pig-bit leg goes stiff and won't bend.

I blink awake.

Not awake, not exactly. I cough against the rotty glamour smell, and when I dart another look into the hall, Acatica is still there—only she's one of those statues made of sand. She's not quite smiling. Rather, it looks like she's just realizing something's not going her way. The bowl is positioned on her outstretched, sculpted hands.

We don't care for your trickery, whisper the walls. *We'll shut you up good.*

"Forgive me," I whisper to Acatica, because there's nothing I can do and I'm trying not to cry as I hurry down the corridor, past each doorway and its span of orange light. The ache in my leg subsides into stinging. My belly hurts, and not just from going hungry for a while. I get to the stairs and take them two at a time.

When I reach the top, my heart lurches. A hallway stretches out so long I can't see the end. Every ten paces there's a door. They line both sides of the corridor, each one smooth and green and twice as tall as me. I'll have to try every one. Into eternity.

The walls giggle.

I close my eyes. I think of Woolpit, its sprawling fields and rolling heath. My little house at the end of the path, its fence that won't stay up and the shed that's perfect for playing pretend in. Glory when we were both small, how she and I would spend hours in the greenwood with berry baskets, discussing whether it's possible to break a dirt clod into such tiny pieces that it would stop being a dirt clod, only it's not Glory's face I see but Acatica's, only that makes no sense because Acatica hasn't been above the mountain in so many *when*s I can't even count them.

Something hisses, and suddenly I'm in Woolpit in February, the endless days of harsh, stinging sleet, the rawness of a nose that won't stop running. The chill of the house, its leaky roof, its elbow-rubbing closeness with a da who farts. Glory Miller, smirking and turning away, giggling behind cupped hands with Kate and Tabby. The whispers about my first ma, what she must have been and done.

My words will never turn as graceful as the wind. My first ma might be a pig. But I am the girl in this story and that means this is *my* story. That means I'm the one who's telling it.

My da, somehow coming up with a bit of mutton in the darkest part of winter to liven up a pot of porridge. My ma, who faces down the gossipy mas of Woolpit who still mutter from the sides of their mouths about foundlings and belonging. Mother the pig, who always seems to know just where I am, even when I have no juicy parsnip tops for her. Mother, who bit me so I may not always be able to see through the seeming, but I know when it's happening. I know not to believe it.

Mother, who never for a moment left me.

Out of nowhere I crack my forehead on something hard and cold. A mighty wooden door without a mark or a carving at the end of a dim, barely lit passageway. The sounds of music and laughter are gone, and only the faintest green light picks out the frame.

Mother brought me to this place. Or the walls let me come here just so they can trap me forever in a tiny closet while I scream and pound and slowly suffocate. Whatever's behind this door may be my end. Or it might set me free.

The only way to know is to open it.

Glory turns up in the earliest part of the morning, brushing snowflakes from her hood. I'm delighted to see her and invite her in to pass the time. She agrees and takes the spindle I lend her, but she's not on the hearth bench for two turns of the thing before she asks, "Where is Martin?"

"Out playing with the other boys." That line has come out of my mouth so often with the housewives that I say it without thinking, without reaching for the fairy cloth.

"But it's barely sunrise." She says it like she's truly puzzled, but I'm instantly on guard. Glory Miller did not just happen by. She intends to put eyes on Martin.

I force a chuckle. "What I meant is that he's gone to spend the night at a friend's hearth. They were out playing, last I saw."

"You said he was sickly." A question creeps into her voice that I have no liking for. "That he stays close to home."

I have to put a stop to this. I pull the fairy cloth all the *way out of my apron and wring it like a dishrag. "Martin is no concern of yours. There's no need to keep looking for him."*

She winces hard like I slapped her, and when at length she blinks at me, thin bands of green stripe one by one through the blue of her eyes. ". . . keep looking for him . . ."

"Right. No need for that. He's always somewhere nearby." I slip the fairy cloth away, then adjust the spindle in her limp hands. "Here, you should spin awhile."

"My da is having trouble finding the green land and the river," Glory says dreamily. "The nearest river is far, far away. Too far for you to walk, he says. Not while you were so sick and weak. Not with Martin so little."

"I can only tell you what I remember." I keep smiling. Brittle and rigid.

"Too far from the wolf pit as well!" Glory sings, but playful instead of mean.

The reeve is going to be trouble. He wants me back with my parents, and that is impossible. Soon enough, the lord of this place will force him to stop looking. The reeve will not be able say to his chieftain nay. I'll be taken away from the ma and da I've fought so hard to make my own.

Chore by chore. Errand by errand. I'll need every one of these people to stand for me. I'll need every housewife and husbandman to circle around Agnes and insist that she has always been here and should not be made to leave.

There is a feast at the manor house. A midwinter feast, even if the villagers use it also to celebrate the birth of their god. There are tables of meat and bread, even a pile of honey cake, and I eat three heaping plates one after another because I can. Already daylight is falling and a massive fire throws shadows everywhere. The whole village is here and the mas pet my hair while the little ones swarm cheerfully, hoping for a piggyback ride.

I am dozens of chores and hundreds of errands beyond the wide-eyed children who dared one another to bump against me to see if my touch would turn them green. The mas are happy to let me swing this child in a dizzying, giggling circle and play-punch that one on the shoulder. All the little ones love Agnes.

I weave through the villagers, looking for Kate and Tabby. After a few moments in my company, they are suddenly going to want to play their favorite divination game, and they will seek out Glory and invite her to play. Then I will happen upon the three of them and—how about that!—they will invite me to join in. These things will happen with just the barest wisp of direction. By spring I can be done with the boy-thing's fairy cloth. I can bury it and forget I ever put hands on it to make this place love me.

Glory appears at my elbow, smiling in a way that sets me on edge. There are more streaks of green in the blue of her eyes. "Come this way. Hurry."

"Why? What's wrong?"

"I'm saving you from them." Glory gestures to Ma and Da near the fire, each holding a mug of ale and smiling at some joke. "Something's happened to Martin. You could very well be next."

I go cold all over. I was not careful with the glamour. This is exactly what the boy-thing wanted—to tempt me to use something that could only lead to ruin.

"Milord says you can stay here at the manor house if you're frightened," she adds.

"No!" I flinch, then frown. "You've spoken to him about this?"

"He thinks it's really the best place for you both," Glory says. "If you live at the manor house, I can come visit. I can stay overnight. You'll have pretty gowns. Mayhap you'll give me one."

No. No. This is all wrong. "Glory, listen to me. The boy is fine. There's no need for any of this."

"If Walter and Matilda hang, you'll have to go live at the manor house," Glory muses.

Like the lord of this place wanted from the beginning. Green children will make him the talk of the other lords, and chieftains have not changed much. Glory Miller is the reeve's daughter, and it's in the reeve's power to hold an inquest into a disappearance. It will be the chieftain who decides fault—and punishment.

"I will never live here," I growl.

Glory studies me for a long moment. Her eyes are more green than blue. "You have to. It's the only way you'll be safe."

Before I can reply, Glory lets out a long, wailing screech that brings the chatter and cheer to an abrupt, shattery halt. "I call hue and cry on Walter and Matilda! Their fosterling's been gone since the harvest and no one's seen him!"

I squeeze my eyes shut. All that work, gone in an instant. I should have buried this wretched fairy cloth when I had the chance. Now Glory is glamourstruck and all she believes is the last thing she was sure of—a small, helpless boy is missing.

She lost her brother. She's going to see to it that I don't lose mine.

The reeve steps out of the crowd, holding a mug and frowning. "Glory, have you gone mad? Martin is playing with the other boys."

"He is not!" Glory gestures angrily. "He's nowhere to be found and—"

"I saw him earlier today," says a ma.

"He was throwing stones with Peter and Dicken on the heath," adds another.

I slowly pull in a breath and dare a sidelong glance. Woolpit is nodding. People are looking bewildered and a little peeved. These people don't get many chances to feast and drink on someone else's coin, and here is Glory

Miller ruining it with accusations that no one believes.

"That is enough, my girl," the reeve says sternly.

Glory stabs a finger at him. "Do your job, Da."

There's a startled murmur, a series of gasps. The reeve's whole face goes stony and he says through his teeth, "Very well."

In two paces, he's at Glory's side. He hauls her screaming and squawking out of the ring of firelight and into the dim. Her voice grows quieter and eventually dies away. My ma and da are looking baffled and worried, and a crowd of their neighbors gathers around them to murmur comfortingly and wonder.

I go sit with Kate and Tabby and play their chestnuts-and-fire game. They are quite eager to see which of them will marry last year's May King, and they get snippy over whose chestnut moves first in the flames. It isn't long before we hear the clanging of tiny bells, and Glory staggers into the firelight, held firmly by her da. Her face is striped by the bars of a huge metal mask and streaked with tears. Her eyes are red and raw, her pale cheeks fiery, but she says nothing. The reeve's grip is sure, wrinkling her dress, but he looks ready to cry, too.

"Glory Miller will wear the mask for a fortnight." The reeve's voice wavers, and he clears his throat. "For bearing false witness against Walter and Matilda."

He looses her with a jangle. Glory stumbles a step, then freezes. The reeve walks away without a glance, but he's *the only one not looking at her. The rest of Woolpit clucks and shakes its head, tsk-tsk, and Glory Miller stands alone at the feast, growing slowly more furious in the flickering light.*

The door swings soundlessly open when I step forward. I don't even have to whisper *once upon a time*.

I'm . . . outside?

I'm more than outside. I'm deep in the greenwood, and around me soar mighty, ancient trees. It's quiet here, eerily so, without birdsong or the rustle of wind or even the lulling buzz of insects. I've never been more than a stone's throw into the greenwood. There's no benefit in it, and plenty of risk. Hunting the king's deer is forbidden, even in the hungriest of times, and the milords of Saint Edmund's and the milords of the countryside still do not agree on who may put the rabbits and birds on their tables. Instead there are bandits and thieves, wolves and badgers, and Those Good People.

The kingdom under the mountain is only a small part of the Otherworld, Granny would say. *All of it is treacherous. It will not want to let you go.*

I turn slowly, trying to work out where I am, but the towering wooden door I just went through is gone. There's a sprawling oak there now, its branches like old bones, crooked and pointy, its acorns in sharp pieces beneath my feet.

There's nothing like a path anywhere, only bushy undergrowth that stretches beneath an endless span of trees.

A chill runs down my back.

This isn't the greenwood. Not *my* greenwood. I'm still in the Otherworld. I must find the wolf pit. That's how I got here, so that's how I can get home. It won't be long before Em comes after me raging, and she will do everything she can to snatch me back under the mountain and trap me there forever. The moment I get home, I must anchor myself. Salt and iron won't work. Because of Senna, I owe something to Those Good People, and they can only be warded away if there's no debt to collect. But she's the only person who may have any idea how to foil a snatching, and she may not want to tell me.

There are two girls in this story now, whether I like it or not, and this is the part where they'd start arguing. They would yell about fault and blame while a shadowy menace creeps up on them both.

I start walking. Tiny glints of wind whisper through the trees here and there, but slippery, like the silvery flash on a frozen puddle. I hurry after them. They're all I have in an Otherworld that won't want me to leave.

I'm on top of the wolf pit almost before I can stop. I skid hard, arms flailing, but only clods of earth tumble toward the shadows at the bottom. The pit looks deeper than I remember, and darker. Overhead, oaks that look bigger and older than the Woolpit trees block out the sky, but for the tiniest peeps of twilit greenish-gray.

I've got to go down there. It's the only way home. But if I can't work out how to cross, I won't be able to climb out of the pit on my own. Em will find me and there'll be nowhere to hide.

Or she won't. I could starve instead. Like those wolves, pacing and whining and finally collapsing, and my white bones would slowly sink into the earth.

The wind must have led me here for a reason, so I swallow hard, lower myself belly-down onto the edge of the pit, and crawl in backward. My feet don't touch the bottom, so I make myself let go and slide what feels like leagues, my dress riding up and my bare legs scraping the cold, jaggedy ground.

My hands are pale against the pit walls, but there's the unmistakable pattern of earth on them. It's like when you lean too long against a haymow and the weave of it stays pressed into your legs. Some of Em's glamour is still on me. Just like Mother when she made her escape. I run my fingers over the uneven, stubbly sides. There's a ripple of movement farther down and

I stop cold. Mayhap Those Good People won't get a chance to trap me. Mayhap I'll be torn apart by a desperate wolf instead.

It's not a wolf, though. It's a rope.

A rope hangs over the opposite side of the pit and there are knots tied every arm's length, like it was made to be climbed. I don't hesitate. I'm up and out of the pit in a trice. I stumble a few tottery steps away from the greenwood and—

I'm on the heath. The Woolpit heath.

My hands are sun-browned and cut across the palms from the wheat field. But there are no patterns. No marks.

My eyes are burning. The heath is blurry and it's a good thing I know it well. I cannot run fast enough. My ma and da will be worried, but I'll say I got lost in the greenwood. It's kind of true. They'll be angry I ventured there, especially when everyone must help at the harvest, but after the scoldings and the smackings they'll forgive me. I'm their baby. Like I was born to them.

But first I must find Senna. It won't do a lick of good to hug my parents if Em can simply snatch me back under the mountain. Senna made this bargain. It's her mess to clean up, not mine.

I am *home*.

No way am I still in the Otherworld, not with the sky that cheerful blue and packed with clouds like sheep on the common. Not with how the leaves on the oaks and elms are such a lively green—

Green. I left at the harvest, when the leaves were turning. Red and brown flying everywhere, crunching underfoot. The air smelling heavy, like wheat chaff and sweat. Not delicate growing things and new flowers opening every day. Those Good People feast and revel every night, and I passed only days down there.

At least it seemed like days.

There's someone crouching at the bottom of the path that leads up to my house, unmoving like a toadstool. Despite the sun, she's bundled in a heavy cloak. It's . . . Glory?

All at once it doesn't matter that she's angry at me. How she repeats whatever Kate and Tabby think on just about everything. She's been worried. That's why she's waiting here. So she'll be the first to know when I get home.

Glory sees me coming and climbs to her feet. Her dress is mucky to the knees, and her yellow hair is a thickety tangle of straw and mud. She peers at me so intently that I stop mid-hug and draw back.

"I know you from somewhere, don't I?" Glory asks in a strange, cautious voice. "From one of the fairs at the abbey?"

"No. I'm Agnes." It sounds strange to say aloud. "Your friend."

"I do have a friend named Agnes, but she looks nothing like you." Glory frowns. There's a faint red line across her forehead, like an old scar that's healing. "She's in danger, but no one believes me. I'm the only one who can keep her safe. I keep watch on her house now."

She gestures up the track, to the smudge of thatch and wattle that's my home.

"The girl who lives there," I say uncertainly. "The one who's green?"

Glory nods. "Agnes."

For the first time in what feels like forever, I have to fight to make words line up in my head. "Glory, it's me. It's Agnes. The other girl is not. Not me. *I'm* me. That other girl is called Senna, and she's one of the Trinovantes and she's not from *now*. She's from sometime long ago before any of our grannies' grannies were here. Her people were being killed by men from Rome, and the king under the mountain offered her a bargain, that if she agreed to serve Those Good People, she'd get to live. Only she must not have thought it through, because it's as bad down there as all the stories say, so she tricked him somehow and . . ."

I trail off as the rotty smell drifts by like a breeze. There's only one reason I'd be smelling glamour, and it means I absolutely cannot spend one more moment talking to Glory. Senna must help me and it must be *now*.

But when I try to dodge past Glory, she grabs my elbow and pulls me up short. "No. I do remember you, Fair Agnes. You were always following me around. Never taking the hint that you weren't wanted."

It hits me square. She can't mean it. It's the glamour. It has to be.

"You humiliated me in front of the May King and my friends at the Maying last year," Glory goes on, redoubling her grip and wrenching me closer, "and you killed my brother because you can't stand it when no one's paying you any mind."

Kate and Tabby were not your friends, I want to say, *and we were there together with baby Hugh. Neither of us put the poker across the cradle.*

The smell is stronger now, as heavy as Glory's grip. Her eyes should be blue but instead they're the same deep, vivid green as Senna's cloak. As the light in the kingdom under the mountain.

"Yes," Glory whispers. "Yes, I remember. You're the one who killed that poor green boy and then fled to hide your crime."

"*Killed* him? I—*what?*"

"Then where were you? Almost a year you've been away, and if you're alive to return, someone was keeping you." Glory says it like there was something amiss with the keeping I must have had, and I shudder.

"Almost a *year?*" I whisper.

"You did poor Martin in at the harvest," Glory replies coldly. "It's nearly May Eve."

There is no time beneath the mountain, Granny would say. *A day can last a year, or a year can go by in an instant.*

When spills out before me. Under the mountain there were two revels. Two days and two nights, and here there were days and se'ennights and months. Of course they think something happened to Martin.

But what about me?

"I did nothing to him!" I struggle, but Glory's grip is iron. The house at the top of the path stands silent. No one comes out to see what's going on.

"Martin disappeared at the same time you did," Glory says through her teeth, "and children do seem to suffer when they're in your care, Agnes Walter. Besides, if you did nothing to him, where is he? And don't you dare tell me he's *just playing nearby.*"

The truth will sound like a tale. Girls don't simply disappear and then reappear out of nowhere without a scratch on them. Boys don't vanish without a trace. I need a story and it can't be the truth.

"He . . ." I cast about as words go everywhichway. "He's gone."

"Gone?" Glory pulls in a harsh breath. "So you admit it. You killed him."

"No, he—"

"Whoever was keeping you killed him," Glory cuts

in, "and you helped. Now you've come back, blood all over your hands, and you think Milord won't stretch your neck? Even if he doesn't, do you think Woolpit will just let you *stay*?"

My heart is rabbiting everywhere. One wrong word and I'll be dragged before Milord. Glory's da is the reeve. He's put the mask on me before. I can absolutely see him in a black hood, dropping a noose over my neck.

"I was with him," I blurt, "in his land. I swear it."

"Martin?" Glory echoes. "You were in . . . Martin's land?"

I nod frantically. "Where I left him. Alive. He's fine. I didn't kill anyone, least of all him!"

"The green land with the river? Where it's always twilight?"

I keep nodding, even though she's describing the Otherworld where the kingdom under the mountain is and Woolpit is still wary enough to think carefully on who and what the green children are.

But I've been gone for almost a year, and a lot can change in all that time.

Glory has been silently staring at nothing for several long moments, so I venture, "All is well now, right? Nothing's happened to Martin. He's where he belongs. So mayhap you could let me go? If I've been away so long, my ma and da must be frantic."

Glory grips harder. "Oh no. You'll be telling them yourself. They'll believe you."

"Tell them what?" I ask, but she's dragging me up the hill and I'm reeling because *nigh on a year* and what if they think like Glory and they're sure I've been somewhere bad? The Woolpit mas must have shaken this story hard, like a dog with a rabbit in its teeth. "Glory, please, there's no time. I must find Senna. Green Agnes. The girl who lives here. *I'm* the one who's in danger."

Glory is hammering a fist on the door. My ma swings it open, and behind her is my da repairing a kettle, and I'm crying because I'm really and truly home. I'm crying because rats and washing stands and walls made of children and Acatica, who I couldn't save, even though standing next to her made me feel less alone and now that I'm back here there's only Glory, who looks through me. I'm crying too hard to make words happen even though they're bubbling over inside me.

"Tell them!" Glory shakes my elbow hard enough that I collect myself because my ma is frowning in concern and my da has come up behind her, the kettle dangling from one meaty hand.

"Weren't you pulling down wood with Agnes?" my ma asks Glory. "Where is she? Is she all right? You didn't leave her by herself, did you?"

"Ma," I squeak, and I move to throw my arms around her but Glory is holding me fast.

My ma peers at me. "Walter, we know this girl. Who is she?"

Who is she?

I blink hard and manage, "I'm your daughter. Agnes."

"You know what?" My da frowns thoughtfully. "We *did* have a daughter named Agnes who was fair. Something happened to her, though."

"I was away," I reply, just like Granny would, like you speak of someone who's been taken by Those Good People. I say it so they'll hear the story in it. "I came home as soon as I could, and I'm never going away again. Never."

My voice is firm, but Em is on her way right now to snatch me back. I wouldn't be smelling glamour if she wasn't. Only Senna might be able to help.

"A better question is *where is Martin*?" Glory shakes me again and her eerie green eyes have a gleam to them that makes my blood run cold. "You will tell them and you will do it now."

"He's not in Woolpit." I say it fast and low, and the leaf-rot smell whispers up like dust. "He hasn't been here since the harvest."

My da goes white. "But he's playing with the other boys."

I shake my head. My throat is closed and I'm fighting tears.

"I told you so!" Glory hisses. "He's gone! He hasn't been here in almost a year and *you're* the ones who kept saying he was somewhere nearby."

The glamour smell comes on stronger and my ma falls to her knees. She's making a sound, a long, high shriek that stutters in and out of hearing, like someone is pulling part of her out through her guts. Her hands clamp over her head as if she's being beaten. My da kneels and silently puts his arms around her.

"My baby!" Ma wails. "My little son. He's dead. He must be dead."

Glory folds her arms and shakes her head like she's disappointed. But I'm crying. Hard. Sobs from the deepest, most raw parts of me. I'm nobody's baby now.

Senna has seen to that.

Only that's not true. There's Mother. My first ma who never left. I scrub tears out of my eyes and fling myself toward the byre. Many pigs are slaughtered in November because they're costly to feed over winter, but my da has never so much as suggested it. The byre is empty, though. There are new tracks in the mud as if she's walked past, but the straw is fresh and unslept in.

Mother's not here.

My ma is still wailing, my da crouched beside her, holding her. They are weeping for Martin. This is Senna's doing, too. It wasn't enough for her to replace me. She made them think they still had a son named Martin, like the brother I lost.

Glory said Senna lives here now. Calling herself Agnes. She must be nearby. The glamour smell is getting stronger by the moment and that means Em can't be far away. Senna will know how I can stay free. She *has* to know.

As I get near the house, Glory is turning from the door, prim and haughty. "I'll be fetching my da. Now that there's someone who can swear to what I've been saying all along."

There's a surge of that leaf-rot smell, and my da flies past us, bounding across the yard and making a noise like a pup who's just spotted his master.

Martin is walking up the path, growing visible step on step, his hair uncovered, his green tunic spotless, for all the world looking exactly as he did when he peered up at me from the wolf pit all those months ago—a small green boy of eight summers or so, dressed in hunting clothes fine enough for a seat in Milord's hall.

He's come. He'll snatch me back. There's nothing I can do. The ground will open beneath my feet and down I'll go like one of the greedy or the vicious or the innocent in Granny's stories.

Martin flings his arms wide and rushes up the last of the hill. I squinch my eyes shut. Where I'm going is sure to hurt. There's a *whish* of motion past me and—nothing.

So I peek. Just a squint, and there's Da holding Martin in the kind of tight embrace that would squeeze the life out of any mortal child. Martin's eyes flick up and meet mine steady on, and I cannot breathe.

He's taunting me. I won't just be snatched. I'll have to spend the next few instants—days—ages—wondering whether *this* is the moment it'll happen.

"My precious boy," my da sobs, "is it really you? They told us you were gone. We thought the worst and here you are. Thank every saint there is."

"I've only just returned," Martin says in Em's voice, and I step back, for all the good it'll do me.

My ma hurries past me, shoving me out of the way. She's a torrent of skirts and shrieking, and she throws her arms around them both and they are weeping as if they've never before known joy.

"Returned?" Glory is hovering, anxious, wide-eyed. At least she's not running for her da. I reach for her arm but she steps away from me. Just like before.

"There was a cold room made of earth." Martin's voice is a tremble. "A man who said he was a king. He made me kneel on the hard floor and swore I would have nothing unless I did as he ordered. Agnes stood by as they all laughed at me. She left me to my fate and never looked back."

I start to bluster how Martin is lying, how I would never do such terrible things, but I stammer and choke because he's not. The pieces all happened, but they did not follow one another that way. It's true without being true. A story that's not a story. Both and neither.

"She'll deny it." There's a cold smile behind his

whimpery panic, his small hands gripping Da's tunic and his head pressed fearfully into Da's shoulder. The rotty smell is sharp and stinging. "That Agnes Walter will deny every word."

I keep telling myself it only seems, but there's no seeming in my da's dark glare trained on me like I'm in his arrowsight. No seeming in my ma's narrowed red eyes and clenched fists.

Da said Senna was pulling down wood. There are only a few places near Woolpit where that's allowed, and by no means can I stay here. I turn on my heel and run hard.

I'm screaming her name. Both names. Senna and Green Agnes. I don't care who hears. Down the track, straight through the village. The Maypole is up, garlands everywhere, trestle tables standing ready for the feast soon to be laid upon them. Past the well, also hung with flowers. I'm halfway down the mill path and out of breath when Martin steps from behind a tree and into my way.

"She can't help you," he says calmly. "Not where you're going."

"Wait!" I stagger back. "Don't snatch me."

Martin sighs, and in that moment he is all Em. There's a wave of leaf-rot and the ground beneath me begins to glow green.

They cannot be bought and they cannot be reasoned

with, Granny would say, *but sometimes—and only sometimes—they are too proud to believe that they can fall victim to the same sort of trickery they so deeply enjoy.*

"I can get her for you. The pig. The one who escaped."

He frowns. Peers at me. "You're lying."

"I'm not. I swear. Give me one day and I'll bring her to the crossing place."

"I could just take you back right now," Martin says, and the ground beneath my feet starts whispering like the walls, *oh yes, give her to us.* "You and the other one, too. I'd walk in the first row for sure with both of you accounted for."

"Not without the pig." I grip my skirt to keep my hands still. "You still need her, don't you? Someone sent a false pig to make a fool of you to amuse the court."

Martin hisses, all Em. "That *Krrrrrrrrshshshshshsh.* Or the Crown Prince. If I ever find out who did it . . ."

He doesn't suspect me. He doesn't want to believe a mortal thing could trick him. Em or Martin, he still wants things in a way that makes anyone vulnerable.

"The pig is nearby," I go on, and even though there's no way I'd ever really turn Mother over, he must believe I would. "She'll hide from you. You'll never find her on your own. If you could, you'd have done it already. She'll come to me. She knows me."

"Why would you do that? There's nothing in it for you."

"I don't want to be given to the walls," I reply quietly, and my shudder is real. "That's my condition. Snatch me back if you must, but let me serve like the others."

Martin smiles, but there's a hard edge to it, one where something's not quite right. "Very well. You have one day. By sundown tomorrow, both you and the pig will be at the crossing place."

I nod. I'm unsteady on my feet. He's tricking me somehow, but at least I have a day to work out how to stop it. That's more than enough time to find Senna. She made this bargain. There must be some way to unmake it.

The lord of this place gave us leave to pull down firewood. Apparently we did not have permission before, and Da gave me an incredulous look when I told him surely the rule did not apply under the cover of night. His look faded to good humor, ha ha, Agnes, always with the delightful jest, *and he was set to forbid my going out collecting until I told him Glory had invited me and I was only going to keep her company. Then all was fine. As long as I was with a friend and not burdening myself overmuch.*

I smuggle a piece of canvas out of the shed. I will tell him she gave me half of her takings.

Ma and Da are too glamoured to notice that I'm keeping my distance from Glory. Hiding from her, truth be told. After the reeve took the mask off her, she hasn't said a word about the boy-thing being gone. Not in public, anyway. But she's made it her business to follow me everywhere, armed with a poorly sharpened meat knife to protect me from my vicious parents who surely mean me harm. When I found her standing guard outside the yard privy while I was making use of it, I sighed and asked, "Aren't your da and our chieftain still trying to find my parents? In the green place? Beyond the big river?"

Glory smiled. "I'm not sure Milord has ever looked."

It's only a matter of time, then. Chores and errands may not save me.

Today the greenwood is peaceful, busy with the sounds of others pulling down wood, and by the end of the day I can barely drag my haul. The windows of the house are glowing a comforting orange as I walk up the path at eventide. There's no reason for Da to see how much wood I have before I can sneak it onto the pile, so I leave it behind the shed and head inside. There's something delicious on the fire, and perhaps Ma can be persuaded to—

The boy-thing smiles at me from the hearth bench where he is enthroned, Ma and Da kneeling at his elbows.

No. He should not be here. I fulfilled every condition the king laid at my feet. I bought my freedom and I bought it dear.

"Look who's returned!" Ma hugs the boy-thing across the shoulders. "Our dear son. Your brother. Safe from his ordeal."

I force a smile. They should not remember him. He was all but gone from their minds, a distant shadow of a son they once had, one always somewhere else. Slowly I move toward the shelf at the back of the house where I put the iron needles for safekeeping.

"You won't find them," the boy-thing says.

"You cannot speak!"

The boy-thing grins, all teeth. "Now I can."

Ma and Da have barely glanced at me, and I've been gone all day and I'm smudgy and there's a cut on my cheek. No one is fluttering around me, tucking a bowl of supper into my hands and rushing me to the comfort of the fire. I think to rub the fairy cloth, but in the boy-thing's presence it'd be a driplet in a downpour.

"Besides, they'll do you no good," the boy-thing goes on. "There's still a debt to be paid."

"Not from me," I reply, but I have no liking for the look about him.

"Blood must serve. Yours or hers." He raises one taunting brow. "But I think both."

Ma and Da have not moved. It's like they're sleeping with their eyes open, frozen at the boy-thing's elbows. I'm still in the doorway, gripping the frame. "You have someone to serve who shares my blood. Her life for mine. That was the bargain."

"That was the bargain," the boy-thing replies, "until she broke it. Now there are no conditions. Now there is only blood that must serve. Yours and hers."

"She's here," I whisper, and when he smiles the smallest,

slyest bit, I know it for true. The old Agnes somehow escaped the kingdom under the mountain, and she told someone where she'd been. That's the only way the boy-thing would be able to speak, and the sole reason he'd feel bold enough to make a claim on me.

Because he has one. Without the old Agnes serving in my place, I still owe a debt to these fairy wretches.

The boy-thing bares his teeth at me, and the reek of glamour fills the room as Da blinks back to life. He rubs his eyes and scowls at me for the first time in . . . ever. "Where've you been?"

Before I can reply, Ma sighs all in a gust. "Prancing in here after dark and expecting us to keep supper for you? You're lucky we put a roof over your head at all. We get nothing for it, you know."

"Ma," *I whisper.* "Da. Please."

"Seems to me you need a lesson in courtesy," *Da growls.* "Since you think so little of this roof, you can sleep under someone else's tonight."

The boy-thing leans his head against Da's shoulder, and Da puts his arm around him, snug and tight. He has them both well and truly glamoured, and he undid in an instant what took three whole seasons to build. If he hasn't snatched me back already, the boy-thing must be plotting something, and it must involve the old Agnes.

"Go!" *Da bellows, and I startle and blink away tears as I hurry away from the square of cheerful orange light. The* dark shape of the pig byre hulks a stone's throw from the house, and I stumble toward it. Mother hasn't slept in it for months, not since the old Agnes left. At the very least the straw will be warm and dry.

Besides, the old Agnes has clearly been here already. She's seen the boy-thing. She's seen what's become of Ma and Da. If she's going to get anywhere near this house again, she'll head to the one place she's likely to see her pet. She'll come to find Mother, and I'll be waiting.

Woolpit is preparing for the Maying. Boys and girls wrap thick garlands of flowers over doorways and along fences, men pile wood for a massive bonfire, and mas with steamy red faces stand over pots and kettles. Every cheerful smile hurts afresh. It's the Maying already, and it feels like only yesterday we were all sweating in the wheat field.

Senna is nowhere among them. She's not at the mill or in the churchyard. I even risk the heath, just far enough to call to her, but she doesn't come and that's as close as I'm willing to get to the greenwood.

I ask at every door in the village. The Woolpit mas don't know me. Those who can be convinced to open their doors to a stranger peer at me suspiciously, jowls in tight frowns, eyebrows arched. *There is an Agnes,* they say, *but you are not her.*

Senna is Agnes now. All it took was almost a year

away for everyone I know and love to forget I was ever here. My village. My neighbors. Even my own ma and da.

The sun is going down and the nip in the air is getting stronger. I have no cloak and no shoes, snatched away like I was at the height of the harvest when it was hot as blazes. I want like nothing else to go home, to curl up on my ma's lap and let her hold me even though I'm too old for such things. Instead I stand at the bottom of the path, looking up at the orange-glow windows and wishing I hadn't followed that crying in the greenwood all those months ago.

Shadows shift in the pig byre. Mother! I race up the hill, but it's Senna who's settling herself into the straw. I've spent all afternoon trying to find her, the girl who traded my life for hers and shoved me headlong into the wolf pit. Now she's here, and I want to knock her a good one and stand her in front of Martin. Then all this can be over.

But her eyes are red, like she's been crying. She pulls in a long, wavery breath. It stops me. All my urgency. All my worry.

All my anger.

"What's wrong?" I ask, because she is nowhere near a smug, triumphant girl who's spent the last year taking things from me one by one.

"You're here," Senna replies bitterly, "and you shouldn't be. You escaped, so now he'll snatch us both away. It hasn't happened, so you must have promised him something. You don't know what you're dealing with, so you've likely doomed us both."

I slip farther into the byre, out of sight of the house. "I thought to stall him. We have till sundown on the morrow."

"All you've done is make it worse," Senna says. "He'll not stand for you making him look the fool."

Reveal nothing to them, Granny would say. *Never give them your fears, your worries, your pain, your guilt. If you do, they will not hesitate to use it against you.*

Only Martin—Em—has worries too. Senna managed to fool the king under the mountain and win her freedom even with Em sent to keep her from it. Without Mother, Em is stuck in that tiny chamber without her fine clothes. The false pig likely made her a laughingstock and possibly worse besides. Em must have returned as Martin to get revenge the only way that would give her satisfaction, and that's to snatch the pair of us away and punish us publicly, and Mother, to regain some dignity before the court under the mountain.

Senna and I are within easy reach. It's Mother who's tripping Martin up. If he's giving me time to find Mother, it means he cannot find her himself, and snatching us back without her will do him no good.

"What if Martin can't take us back?" I say aloud. "What if we can stop him?"

Senna gives me a hard look. "Are you simple? There's a debt outstanding. There's no stopping him. No salt and iron. No business with food. A bargain made is a bargain sealed."

"That's the thing of it," I reply. "*There's a debt outstanding*. Who owes it?"

"We *both* do," Senna snaps.

"Then . . . isn't it also true that *neither* of us does?"

She starts to say something. Then stops.

"You don't owe it because you fulfilled it," I go on, "and I don't owe it because I never made it in the first place. You owe it because I didn't fulfill it, and I owe it because you passed it on to me."

Senna is slowly nodding. "Both and neither."

"What we need is a new bargain," I say. "One that makes sure we're both free of Those Good People."

"You keep saying *we*," she mutters.

"It has to be we," I reply. "*We* is both you and me at the same time it's neither you nor me. Each of us by ourselves owes a debt and is bound by a bargain. Together we are free of both. At least until tomorrow at sundown."

"Even if I trusted you," Senna says cautiously, "there's no way the king under the mountain will make a new bargain."

"He might, for the same reason anyone takes a bad bargain."

She bristles. "What we'd need to ask for wouldn't be bad. It would be *humiliating*."

"Why? We don't want their treasure. We don't want their favor. All we want is to be free of whatever bargain you made all those years ago."

"That's *not* all we want." Senna sighs, big and windy. "While you're making a bargain with the king under the mountain, he's already thinking of every possible way he can work around it and get what he wants regardless. We must make our demands carefully. At the very least, one condition must be that there'll be no other punishments. No wasting away of a fever. No blight on the wheat."

A blight on the wheat would punish all of Woolpit. Not just us. But if Those Good People feel they're wronged, they will not hesitate.

"We'd be forcing the king under the mountain to accept a new bargain with new conditions that he did not offer and doesn't benefit him. *That's* the humiliation." Senna shakes her head. "We'd have to do something catastrophic to even get his attention. The whole fairy court would have to suffer. They'd have to believe their other choice was death, and I can't begin to imagine what it would take to harm those fairy wretches that much."

"Mayhap." I pull out a set of iron needles that I stole off the door of a Woolpit ma. "But we can make the fairy court suffer. We can keep them from the thing they like best—their fun."

When it gets dark, the old Agnes and I slip out of the pig byre and drift through the village stealing iron needles off doors. By the time we're finished, we have enough needles to fill each of our palms so full that our thumbs don't quite fit around them.

She is telling me a story: Salt and iron ward those fairy wretches away from person, place, or thing, so there will be no snatching anyone under the mountain if they cannot use their crossing place. If the boy-thing cannot get home, if he gets sicker and sicker and cannot call for help, he just may change his mind about the purpose of blood.

We pass a restless night in the pig byre. Neither of us sleeps, and when the barest of gray dawns has lifted, we're on our way to the crossing place. The pit is hidden in a smudge of fog. A lingering length of rope still hangs over the edge, put there by the reeve as a safety measure after the boy-thing and I were found at the bottom. We each fling our needles into the pit, where they make a dull clatter, then the old Agnes climbs down and I follow. She lifts a hand toward the pit wall, not quite touching it, and that's when it hits me, what she means to do.

She means to silence the walls.

Full of iron, they will struggle to think clearly. Full of iron, they will be of no use at all to those fairy wretches.

The old Agnes presses a needle against the dark, crumbling earth. In her other hand, she holds a palm-size rock poised like a hammer. She glances at me, and I steady myself and do likewise. We are a neither-nor. This must be carried out as one. At her nod, each of us drives a needle into the pit wall. The iron disappears slow and even, and tiny trickles of rich black dirt patter our feet.

Stop that, *the walls hiss.* How dare you—

We bring the rocks down till the needles have disappeared into the wall and only the tiniest winks of metal remain. The walls are sputtering, gabbling out threats in broken syllables. The old Agnes leans down, picks up a handful of loose earth, and crams it into the dent left behind.

"This must go quickly," she says. "Before the walls can call for help."

We drive the rest of the needles without speaking. The walls in the kingdom under the mountain are more than just the souls who've been dragged within. They are the eyes and ears of those fairy wretches. The whisper that won't leave you be. But now their hearing has *been muffled. Their vision dimmed. Their vicious mouths gagged and their thoughts muddied. They will not think to carry tales. They will not respond when one of their masters calls upon them.*

They will not know they're needed.

There's a commotion at the house as we're coming up the rise toward the pig byre. Da rushes toward the shed, then back with a double armload of firewood. He should be following the harrow this time of year, and he should already be afield and nowhere near home till evening. The old Agnes and I trade glances and hurry.

"He was fine this morning!" Ma's voice is shrill and scared as she rushes toward the garden. "Where's that chamomile? I know I have some!"

The old Agnes and I edge toward the door and peek in, but Ma and Da are too frantic to pay us mind. The boy-thing lies in their bed, moaning and shivering, with the fire built to roaring and every blanket in the house heaped on him.

"It's happening again," the old Agnes says, and there's a note of triumph in her voice. "I remembered from last time. How sick Martin got just being out from under the mountain."

She still doesn't know I made him ill to force her to make a bad decision in haste, without giving her a chance to think it through. But he got that sick that fast because

I buried iron right beneath him, in the floor of a house where no one owed him anything. It's true enough that those fairy wretches get more ironsick the longer they're above the mountain, but for him to be this ill so soon makes no sense.

Unless the iron in the pit walls is doing this. Unless piercing the very ground we share with the Otherworld has poisoned him.

The old Agnes meant to make the whole fairy court suffer by penning them up so they could not amuse themselves with our sorrows. That they're likely ill as well—it's a downright joy to picture.

Da is by the woodpile. Ma is in the garden. Neither is watching the door, so I slip in and approach the bed. The boy-thing looks bad. *He's such a pale green that he almost looks like a normal boy. His cheeks are sunk deep, like a corpse, and there's a sheen of sweat on his brow.*

My brother's face. Long dead but not forgotten. Never forgotten. I grit my teeth even as I blink hard.

I pick up a rag and bowl of water next to the bed. The old Agnes stations herself on the boy-thing's other side. When I touch the damp cloth to his forehead, his eyes fly open.

"What have you done?" he wheezes.

"Made you sick," the old Agnes replies calmly, "and trapped you here. Once the king under the mountain sets us free, we'll fix it."

The boy-thing's teeth are clattering. "You. Made. A. Bargain."

"Then suffer," I reply, and I wipe his forehead daintily as if I give a tinker's curse whether he gets well or not.

"Once we're released from that bargain," the old Agnes goes on, "both of us, and allowed to live here with our ma and da in peace, I promise we will make things as they were for you. You'll be well again. You can go back to your place and be about your business there."

Our ma and da. Across the bed, the old Agnes— Agnes—is earnest and firm. My throat is closing. From those first moments the king laid out terms, my thoughts went to trickery. How I could hoodwink a girl like me, how I could fool and beguile her. The king left me no choice. Just as he did with that first bargain, me trembling and weeping at his feet.

There was a choice, though. A simple one. A human one. I could have asked for this girl's help and believed she would give it if she could.

Just like I should have believed that Ma and Da would love me without me having to beguile them.

They nearly won, those fairy wretches. I almost ended up no better than them.

The boy-thing sinks back against the bedclothes, panting. He slits his eyes at me. "You think when I die you can still direct my glamour? Oh, don't look so shocked. I could feel what you've been doing to these fools from the moment I crossed. Walter and Matilda don't love you. They never have. You forced them to, and you will lose everything. They will turn you out. Slam the door right in your face and ignore your crying on their doorstep."

I'm holding in panic. The tears that won't stay down. Agnes will have them back, both of them. They will wonder why they ever took this green stranger into their home.

"Or . . ." The boy-thing draws out the word, and then he starts speaking in the tongue of my childhood, the calming swirl of syllables and curlicue words that whisks me back to before Rome left everything in ruins. "The bargain still holds. You could return this dim girl to the pit. I'm too weak to walk, but you could carry me there, and once I touched that earthen floor with her, you'd never see either of us again. You could come home, to this house, and there'd be your ma and da, arms open, like I was never here. The world you crafted with my glamour. Just you and them. You'd have your family back, free and clear."

Agnes is frowning her bewilderment, looking thick as a pudding full of lumps, rot her, because even when weak glamour hits it's hard to blink through it. For three whole heartbeats I decide she will be my sacrifice, and I will shove her in the pit without mercy or afterthought.

But then I'm back in myself, back in this house and back at the side of a girl who has never once thought to do the same to me. I made a bad decision one time when I was afraid. I can't have it back, but I can make a better one now. I fold my arms and regard the boy-thing, weak and squirming under his pile of covers, and I shake my head.

"We've made it so you can't snatch us anywhere," Agnes tells him, "and you cannot call to those like you, either. We are the only ones who can put that right. As far as I'm concerned, you're reaping what you've sown. Now you and your kind must take the sort of bargain you once gave to Senna—agree or die."

The boy-thing flinches each time Agnes says *we*, but when she sits back, he smiles in a cheerful, cheeky way, as if we'd caught him in a bit of mischief. "Very well. I free you from this bargain. Now lift whatever ward you've placed on me before I get so weak I can do nothing for you."

Agnes sits up straighter, but I hold out a hand. "That's not in your power. The king under the mountain made this bargain. Only he can free us from it."

In an instant, the boy-thing's face goes vicious. "And how am I to call him? Hmm? Am I to die here because you've stopped me from doing the very thing that could save me?"

He's right. If he could call to the other fairy wretches, he'd have done it already. We have the wolf by the tail. We cannot hold it forever, but if we let go, we'll be mauled.

"You might be able to keep me from snatching you," the boy-thing sneers, "but iron won't stop my kind from leaving the kingdom under the mountain. The court rides on every holy day. That's May Eve. Tonight. Once they cross, my kind will hear me calling. They will come for you both, and they will have no mercy. Blood must serve, even if it serves to water the dark earth."

I grip the sickbed rag so hard that it dribbles water on the bedclothes.

"When they realize they cannot go home because of whatever you did to the crossing," he goes on, "they will level this village. Every man, woman, and child will bleed into the soil for the insult, and we will make this place our own."

"You cannot," Agnes whispers, but she is remembering that fairy wretches do not lie. She is realizing that her plan to keep them safely contained in the Otherworld will fail.

"Daddy!" the boy-thing cries weakly, batting my rag away with a flail of hand. "Mama! She's hurting me! Help!"

I barely have time to turn before Da's big hand falls on my shoulder and I'm staggering away from the bed. Agnes is backing away on her own, edging toward the door.

"It's her." The boy-thing waves a trembling hand at me. "She's the one who pushed me in the pit. She left me there to die. Daddy, why didn't you come?"

It takes me a moment, because it sounds so much like a lie and the boy-thing cannot lie, not in this form or any other. But oh, gods—I did push him into the wolf pit. Right after I pushed Agnes, all those months ago. When I stood over them victorious, convinced I was finally free of him in every form.

"I'll kill whoever hurt you, son," Da growls. "I'll kill her with my bare hands!"

"Make her go away!" the boy-thing shrieks, and a whiff of glamour rises like horse apples downwind. "The other girl, too. She was there. I bet she helped. Make them both go!"

The iron in the pit walls should be disrupting his glamour if it's making him sick, but he wouldn't need much. Not given how I've been directing Ma and Da all this time. He might even be using the scrap in my apron.

The boy-thing coughs pitifully, writhes in the bedclothes, and rasps out noises that are half cry and half moan. Ma starts bawling and I slither out of Da's grip and fly out the door, where I nearly collide with Agnes. We sprint headlong through the garden, away from our house and away from where Glory is possibly keeping vigil at the bottom of the path.

At last we stop. There are fields on one side of us, greenwood on the other. Agnes sinks against a tree and touches an open wound on the back of her leg below the knee. "I know it's not real. Ma and Da. I know he's magicked them. But what if they don't get better? What if they're like this forever?"

I shake my head. "There are different kinds of seeming. This kind lasts only long enough to cause people to make bad choices, and the source of the glamour must be nearby for it to work."

"So if Martin goes back where he came from, Ma and Da will be like they once were?" She toys with a flower. "Glory, too?"

"Whatever they did when they were glamoured will not change, but they will have no memory of doing it." I make no mention of what it is to be glamourstruck. How there is no coming back from that. "But it won't matter, will it? Those Good People are going to destroy this village. We cannot let the boy-thing summon the king, yet no one but the king can free us from the bargain, and I'm sure as anything not going back down there."

Agnes nods slowly. "The king is going to come to us, though. Those Good People will ride on May Eve."

I scoff. "Ride roughshod over this whole village and leave it a boneyard. They will rise from their sickbeds if that's what it takes, which will only make them more violent."

"Through the crossing place? That's the only spot they can come and go? And the king will lead the ride?"

The tilt of her questions stops me from giving another snide answer. Agnes is running her fingers through the dirt, but she is somewhere far away. At length she holds up a tiny object, pale, all corners. A bone.

"What if we stop him?" Agnes whispers. "What if he must halt the ride and listen to the terms of our new bargain? What if he must accept them if he thinks to leave the Otherworld ever again?"

"I can think of nothing we could do to force him into such a thing," I reply, and this time it comes out kind instead of unhelpful. "Nothing we could offer to tempt him."

"Precious few things gain and hold attention in the Otherworld. One is a bargain." Agnes places the tiny bone between us. "The other is a sacrifice."

pick two bluebells and strip away the blooms. Senna sits across from me. She is no longer as green as the leaves around us, but she seems paler than usual. I snap one stem off halfway and leave the other long.

The loser of this draw will be the sacrifice.

The story will go like this: A girl will climb into a grave at the bottom of the wolf pit. She will hold close to her chest the piece of Martin's cloak that Senna tore when she pushed him in. She swears up, down, and sideways that there's enough glamour in this piece of fairy cloth to keep that girl alive, even buried, and this will fool the king under the mountain. The sacrifice will seem real, and nothing else will compel the king to halt the ride and parley with the girl who is not buried.

The walls have been made quiet with iron. The king will not know what we've done to the crossing place till it's too late.

The girl who is not buried will tell him. *No one but*

me can restore it, she'll say, *and your kind will neither cross here nor get well unless you agree to a new bargain.* The king will have no choice. His kind will be suffering. The crossing place blocked by sacrifice. Once the new bargain is struck, the girl who is not buried will dig up the one who is. She will step out of her own grave, safe and healthy, and they will both be free.

That is the story, but I don't want to be the girl in it. Rather, there's one girl in particular I don't want to be. It has to be one of us, though. It has to be *we* who carry this off.

Senna looks away as I slip the stems behind my back and shuffle them. Tonight is May Eve and Those Good People will ride at midnight. There is no time to dither and argue. I gently press the stems between my hands so neither of us knows which is short and which is long.

Short straw is going in the ground. Long straw will dig.

There have always been bones in the pit. Not all of them wolves. Someone must have done this before. *When* is a very long time.

I offer the stems to Senna. I hold, she chooses. Like every time Glory and I decided who'd hide first in a game of seek-and-find or who had to sweep spiderwebs from the farthest corners of the manor house dairy shed.

Senna hovers two pinchy fingers over one of the stems. Then the other. Woolpit is in terrible danger.

When the king under the mountain is compelled to halt, one of us must be waiting to parley. The other must be beneath the cold soil. Present and absent. Both and neither.

But Senna is surely thinking the same thing I am. *I'm not sure I trust her to dig me up.*

Green fingers flash. Senna pulls a stem from my hands and closes a fist around it. I open my palm so we can both see what's left.

I'm holding the long one. I'm going to dig. Me with my dirty feet and stumbly words, the girl who was never meant to be in any story but an ordinary one.

Senna swallows visibly. She licks her lips and uncurls her fingers, and there's the crumpled stem as long as her thumb. She wads it up and throws it away in one harsh motion.

We are quiet while birds chirr and the wind twists all silvery through the hedge.

At last I say, "We should get a shovel. We must be ready by sundown."

She nods. Evening is day and night, both and neither. There's a shovel in the shed near the house, and we move quickly. The yard is quiet, but Ma's singing drifts out the front door, *lully-lully-sleep-my-baby* like when I was small and down with some fever. We come toward the house the back way, through the garden, and cross the yard to the shed. It's cool and dark within, and Da has moved all the tools around. The shovel isn't where I thought it was, and by the time we find it, a clatter in the yard makes me duck behind the door and pull Senna next to me.

A cart rolls up the rise. The reeve sits on the driver's plank and Glory is next to him. There are knitting needles dangling around her neck on a piece of string. The pair that matches mine, that Granny gave her when we were both small. Ma comes out of the house at the creak of wheels, and the reeve pulls the donkey to a stop.

"Sir Richard has asked me to bring the green children to the manor house." The reeve doesn't climb down, only shades his eyes with one hand while he peers at my ma. "It's been nearly a year and their parents are nowhere to be found. You've taken excellent care of them, but he thinks it's more than time they were off your hands."

"Off my hands, is it?" My ma smirks. Ma *never* smirks. "Into his hands, more likely."

My mouth falls open. It's discourteous to speak rudely to the reeve. *No one* refuses a direct command from Milord.

"They'll come with me now," the reeve says in a no-nonsense way. "Are they inside? Bid them get in the cart."

"You will not take my boy from me. You have no right!"

"Sir Richard has every right," the reeve says patiently. "They are foundlings, and he has a duty to their welfare, and yours, too."

"Their *welfare*?" My ma scoffs. "He wants to put them on display as a curiosity. Imagine who'd come to have a look at green children. First among them would be those pompous men he's always trying to impress with his worldliness. He'd finally be the talk of the countryside, wouldn't he?"

The leaf-rot smell drifts from the house, and my pig bite hurts. Glamour. Of course. It's making Ma say such terrible things about Milord and his motives, and rudely, too. Even if those things are not exactly untrue. Martin is sick, yet he's still trying to ruin my family out of spite. Any moment now the reeve will be glamoured enough to drag Ma before Milord, where she'd be fined for slander.

"Da," Glory says in a low, urgent voice, "we have to take them now. That Fair Agnes is lurking somewhere. She'll be the reason they go back to that room made of earth. Martin said as much."

"You cannot take Martin anywhere," my ma retorts. "He's ill. Come look for yourself if you don't believe."

Glory's eyes go wide and she scrambles off the cart, flies past my ma, and leans into the house. From the doorway she shouts, "Da! Fair Agnes has done something horrible to him! I want to call hue and—"

"*Hush now*, Glory Miller!" the reeve bellows, loud enough that even I jump. "Remember we talked about these notions of yours. The boy is simply ill. Get back on this cart right now."

Glory makes one last helpless, frantic gesture at Martin's sickbed, but she does as she's told, needles clicking. She slumps next to her da, worrying a thumbnail. *You're right,* I want to tell her. *I've done this to him. But he's not a boy, and he's the one you should fear.*

A year ago I could have done it. A year ago it would have been Glory and me facing down Martin and the raging host that'll ride on Woolpit at midnight.

"The boy can stay till he recovers. I'll be back to check on him in a se'ennight's time." The reeve glances around the yard. "Is the green girl sick as well?"

My ma huffs a fierce sigh. "That girl. Take her! I've had enough of her wantonness."

"Is she home? Where can I find her?"

"I don't know where she is, and I care less. I've half a mind to call hue and cry on her myself. She threw my precious boy into the wolf pit and left him there to starve." Ma scowls. "A little honest work will do her some good. If you can find her, take her to the manor house with my blessing."

Senna lets out a long, trembly breath. Her whole attention is on my ma and there are tears in her eyes. Almost a year Senna's been here, being me. Her own ma and da are ages gone. She doesn't even have a Mother. But for my parents, she has no one.

But for me, who once thought to be her foster sister and friend.

The reeve squints at my ma. "Then surely you won't mind if I look around here a little."

"Of course not. Now I must go. My poor boy needs me."

Senna and I trade looks. Neither of us is anyone's baby, not as long as Martin is here. The reeve climbs off the cart and walks toward the garden behind the house. Glory is still on the seat, her back to us. Senna grips the shovel and eases the shed door open.

We go together, hurrying down the path. Senna makes it to the bottom unseen and slips behind the hedge, but Glory must hear my footfalls because she turns and spots me and lets out a wordless screech. I freeze. The reeve may or may not march me before Milord and argue to hang me, but he'll keep me long enough that it won't matter. There will be no sacrifice and no parley with the king under the mountain.

Woolpit will be doomed, and Senna and I with it.

Glory is taller than I remember. She must have grown while I was away. But she is still Glory. We lost our first milk teeth on the same day. We once had matching hair ribbons, given to us by a merchant on the road to the abbey who we convinced we were twins. It's the glamour making her cruel and vengeful.

Please have Glory be the kind of friend she used to be. I thought to ask it of Senna and Martin when I was sure they owed me a favor. Days ago, months ago, *when ago.* I wouldn't have thought to ask if it was only glamour.

"Martin is worth ten of you," Glory says, low and vicious, "and proof be hanged, I will see that you pay for what you've done—"

The reeve grabs Glory around the middle and clamps his other hand over her mouth. He glances at me, but he's too busy muffling her ravings to pay me mind as he marches her toward the cart.

"Please don't make me put the mask on you again, my girl," he mutters, and there is a rawness that makes me think of my first da who is a washing stand, who I ended up leaving alone after all. "Enough with these stories, I beg you."

Glory will be back to her old self if Senna and I can do our work tonight, but mayhap it ought to be my turn to be the best dog namer, straw braider, and butterfly chaser in Woolpit. Mayhap it'll be better for Glory to go turn heads with Kate and Tabby if that's what she really wants.

Only then I'll have no one. I'll have to braid straw and chase butterflies by myself.

I'm not alone today, though. I meet Senna at the bottom of the track where it meets the main path, and she walks at my elbow, chin up, intent. Senna and I, who are *we*.

I t's late afternoon by the time we reach the pit. We light a small fire at the bottom to help us see. There's one shovel, so we take turns digging. Ten stabs for me, ten for her. The dirt we heap carefully nearby. The bones we fling into the shadows so neither of us must look at them. As the sun is disappearing, Agnes and I stand on either end of a hole that's an arm's length wide, a girl's length tall, and just over knee-deep.

It's everything I can do to keep my face serene. I'm not worried I won't survive. The fairy cloth will keep me safe. What it can't do is move this dirt off me if Agnes decides to walk away and leave me here.

I will stay in this grave, fully alive, buried forever.

Agnes squints at the setting sun. Time has come. Twilight is the neither-nor those fairy wretches love so much. They're drawn to anything that is not entirely one thing or another, but are both and neither at once. This time it'll bite them right in the sitting place. This time it means we can win.

Still, it's slowly that I step into the hole. Slowly that I lie down. Slowly that I help Agnes place the first few sturdy branches meant to keep the weight of the dirt off me. She's been saying *we* this whole time. Like there's no other way to be. I have to believe she means it.

The ground beneath me is cold, even for a pit at nightfall. There are bones here for a reason. This is a place that's been here longer than both of us. Agnes's round bread-dough face hovers over me. She holds the shovel with a resolve I did not expect from her. Quietly she says, "It's not real. It only seems."

"See you soon," I say, and I meet her eyes as she lays the last few branches over my face, then drapes a scrap of canvas over them. The world goes dark and I swallow a whimper. I fold my arms over my chest as if I really were a corpse. In my right hand I clutch the fairy cloth.

There's a shick of metal on dirt, then a pattering weight drops on the branches at my feet. A handful of earth tumbles through the small cracks and rains on my legs. Agnes is filling in the hole. Another shovelful falls, then another. The air is getting heavier. Never so heavy that I can't breathe, but enough that I dare not move.

My knuckles whitening around that green whisper of cloth are the last thing I see as Agnes heaps dirt over the branches and canvas covering my head.

t's done.

My hands are shaking. My belly churning. The hole we dug is now a patch of dirt slightly raised above the pit floor, and Senna is at the bottom of it.

There's nothing to do but wait.

When Those Good People ride, it will be at midnight, Granny would say. *Be in your bed with the covers pulled tight and you'll be safe till morning.*

Only I'm sitting on the edge of the wolf pit, my legs dangling down, so I'm neither in nor out. I've taken off my dress and I'm wearing just my undershift, so I'm neither clothed nor naked. My hair is half braided, half in tails. I am both and neither. I am me and we.

That patch of ground is so still. Like Senna is truly dead and slowly turning to bones in the cold earth.

I sit on both hands to keep from rushing to help her. It's trickery. For a trick to work it must look real.

The fire we built at the bottom of the pit slowly

fades to coals, then goes out entirely. I dare not climb down and stoke it. The moment I leave neither-nor, we are no longer we. The dark grows deep and thick and cold. I've never been out alone this late, and I don't like it. I'd rather be at the Maying. This year I'd be a better friend. I would think to ask before I approached the May King for someone who really might not want her private feelings aired.

The rotty smell rises and all at once I *am* at the Maying, and it's music and dancing and heaping boards of food, but this time I'm ready for it. The glamour works its way into my eyes as Those Good People stir in the Otherworld, but I can blink it away. The sting of pain from the bite on my leg helps me keep myself in myself and not go all fuzzy.

Mother is with me even here.

he walls are delirious. They are whispering all their fever dreams to me, shot through with iron like they are, and at first I'm afraid that they'll pull me in and Agnes will dig up an empty grave, if she digs me up at all.

But then I start listening.

My ma made the best roast.

My sweetheart's brother is wed to your cousin. That makes us kin.

My grandda inked these marks on my back.

They are still here. Trinovantes, Iceni, Cantiaci, Catuvellauni—alive in whispers. Alive in the stories we told to the rocks and flowers, because no one is really gone. They remain in the smallest ways, if only you know how to listen.

y leg hurts sharp and stabby at the same moment a gust of glamour hits me hard enough to ruffle my hair. There's a rumble coming at me too, like a whole courtful of horses pummeling my way from the blackest part of the wolf pit where I can't see. They're bearing down on me and they'll leap up from the pit bottom and trample me and I must move out of the way if I want to live.

"St-stop." My voice fills the dark of the greenwood, the empty silence of a night I should not be out in. There can be no kneeling and no fear. No stumbly words. "I would parley with the king under the mountain. I call upon him to heed my sacrifice and halt."

The hoof-rumble stops abruptly. It's too dark for me to see the bottom of the pit anymore, but the sound of restless horses and the clink of bits and stirrups fills the shadows. My arm hairs are prickling and I can barely breathe.

A green light bursts out of the darkness and throws gaping shadows on all sides of the pit. The king under the mountain is standing on Senna's grave, holding the reins of a massive black horse. He's dressed to ride, but he's sweaty and pale. His glare is absolutely murderous in the moment before a false, polite smile takes him over.

"Of course it'd be you," says the king. "More clever than you look. I thought for sure that useless fool would turn you into a looking glass or a privy seat and save me the trouble. I should have known she'd make the same mistake again."

He's talking about Em. That's why he sent me to find her with that butterfly. I was never supposed to walk out of her little room.

"I didn't think you'd have the stomach for a proper sacrifice, though." The king tamps the ground with one boot. "You know enough to compel me, but I can't imagine any reason you would want to. It'll do no good to plead for mercy."

"I don't want mercy," I reply. "I'll have no need for it once you agree to a new bargain."

The king laughs aloud and waves a hand. There's a surge of horse-noise, hooves and whinnying and the creak of leather, but it's jammed up and anxious, like horses and riders penned in. The king lifts raging eyes to me, and I fight down the urge to grin.

"What have you done?" he asks in a low, dangerous

voice, but the menace is broken when he coughs, hard and hacking.

"Some things may have been misplaced nearby." I gesture around, intentionally vague, giving him nothing he can use against me. "You may feel . . . unwell."

"Sacrifice cannot compel me forever." The king scrubs a hand over his damp forehead. "I can wait far longer than you."

"True enough. You can wait till I die, and ride over my bones. But once you do, you won't ride home again. You'll be stuck in this dismal, mortal world, dying slowly from the salt and iron."

The king buzzes something low and threatening.

"And mayhap you've noticed one of your own missing. The *useless fool* who couldn't even turn me into a privy seat. Oh yes," I go on as the king stiffens with fury, "if you were waiting for the walls to whisper to you, I made them quiet. They'll stay quiet forever, and the useless fool will die trapped above the mountain with anyone who rides tonight. He's called Martin here and he's a boy, just like he appeared that first time. Even now he's ironsick and getting worse. Likely because of the things that got misplaced nearby. Would you like to reconsider striking a new bargain?"

The king buzzes again, viciously. The green light casts long, dancing shadows in the pit, and the piled earth from Senna's grave laps at his boots. However he feels about Em, it will make him look weak if she dies at the hands of mortal girl-things. At length he says, "I'm listening."

Those Good People will honor a bargain, but they hate to lose. Even now the king is scheming a way to snatch us back regardless. Senna said as much. Every last part of this must be just right.

"Senna and I will be free from whatever bargain you made with her all those years ago." My words are coming clear and strong, no hint of a tangle. "She and I will be allowed to live here, with our ma and da, and neither you nor any of your kind will trouble us or anyone in Woolpit in any way. In return, we'll find all the misplaced things so the crossing place won't make you sick, and you may use it freely. You can take back the one I know as Martin so he can get well."

The king under the mountain shifts and paces, but he never leaves the square of earth where Senna is buried. I hope she cannot feel it, down there in the dark.

"Blood must serve," the king says at last. "I cannot agree to those terms."

There's a rumble of horse-noise, dim, as if Those Good People hidden by shadows tried one more time to push past the iron holding them back.

"That is the bargain." I dig my fingers into the pit edge. "Take it and ride, or leave it and rot."

The king starts buzzing, harsh and angry, and he

stomps around on Senna's grave like he's being stung. "Fine. Fine! You and the girl-thing shall have your liberty of us."

"Senna," I prod, because he must have no way to slither around his word. "The girl you turned green to punish."

"You and Senna, then. All other blood must serve." The king hides another cough in a growl. "And you will undo whatever mischief was done to this place that keeps us from our rightful ride."

Acatica is still in the Otherworld. My da, all alone. But there's no other way. I swallow hard and nod.

"Say it aloud if you agree!" the king roars, and in the shadows a thudding of hooves makes me jump. "A bargain isn't a bargain till it's made and sealed!"

"I agree to those terms." I say it quick before he can take back the offer. Before I lose my nerve.

In a blink, the king's whole manner changes. He's still ashen-sick but he grins big, like a wolf, and makes a come-here gesture to me. There's no way I'm moving from the pit edge, but there's a rustling behind me and Mother steps out from the greenwood.

All other blood must serve. Mother is one of the Trinovantes, same as Senna. Same as me.

"No," I whisper, but it's too late. Mother is moving toward the king like she's being guided unresisting on a leash.

Her every step is familiar. The bob of her shoulders. The swing of her rump. The bounce of her ears. But as Mother nears the pit edge, she glows faintly green and ripples and shifts and changes. Her middle grows thinner and her legs thicker and her head pulls into a round human shape, and a curtain of hair that's fair like mine swishes down her back.

When Mother gets to the edge of the pit, she leaps. I cry out—it's deeper than it looks, more than enough to turn an ankle or worse—and only at the last moment do I remember that I can't slide in and chase her. I can't leave neither-nor.

"Mother." I mean to yell it. To scream after her, to beg her to come back just long enough to hold her hands up so I can brush her fingers in something like a hug. Even a moment would be a gift. But the word comes out strangled. Like all my guts are twisted up and keeping *Mother* trapped in the choke in my throat.

She lands lightly, gracefully, and then she's at the elbow of the king under the mountain and he's grinning as he drapes a thick green cloak over her bare shoulders.

I'm too stunned to move. Too angry to cry. I've been tricked again and now I've lost Mother forever.

"Mother!" My voice grinds to life. I don't care how the words sound. I'm going to shout them. "Mother, it's me! I—I know what happened. Thank you. For everything. I love you!"

Mother's eyes go big. Both hands fly to her mouth. She's younger than my Woolpit ma, no silver in her hair. She starts toward me, but the king's green cloak over her shoulders holds her where she is. She can't even free a hand enough to wave.

"I'm sorry," I whisper, because I've already left so many people behind and now one more, the one I love most, is slipping through my fingers.

Her mouth is moving, but no words are coming out. She paws at her throat while at her elbow the king lifts one taunting brow.

"Da's waiting for you." My voice is raspy and my eyes sting. "He misses you. Please, just go be with him."

Mother looks up. A faint ripple of hope softens the helpless lines in her face, and she nods once, firmly.

They will have each other, at least. Mother will sit by my da in that crystal room so he won't always be alone.

"Farewell, girl-thing. Till next time." The king under the mountain makes a mocking half-bow and takes Mother by the elbow. Together they walk out of the green light and disappear into the darkness of the pit. The horse-noise and leather-squeal fade as well, clattering into the shadows till there's nothing left but stillness.

Night sounds take over the greenwood once more. All is dark and silent.

Till next time. But there won't be a next time. A bargain

made is a bargain sealed, and I bought us freedom, Senna and me.

All it cost was Mother.

I swipe away tears and glare at the patch of raised dirt, trampled over and through with boot prints. Mother is gone, and it's Senna's fault. None of this would be happening if Senna hadn't lured me in the first place. I'd still have my ma and da, and even if Woolpit didn't think much of me, they'd know me. Senna took my parents. She stepped square into *Agnes* as if there was no first Agnes who had to suffer in her place. Senna took Mother as sure as if she'd called her from the pit edge herself.

I could leave Senna in the ground. No one would ever know.

Only without Senna, I would never have been the girl in the story. I'd have gone on with the harvest, my hands covered with cuts atop cuts, and there'd have been milking and spinning and Glory looking down her nose at me. All very safe things. All very ordinary. Because of Senna there's a whole new story, one I never thought could even exist, much less with me in it.

I grab the shovel and slide on my belly into the pit.

t's dawn when I step out of my grave. Neither night nor morning. I take Agnes's hand and she hauls me up staggering, dirt raining off me. For long moments I just sit and breathe. It's chilly, though, and before long I'm up and rubbing my arms and jigging in place.

"Let's be gone from here," I say, and Agnes nods but doesn't move. She's sickbed-pale and picking at her collar. "You all right?"

She shakes her head. "Mother. He took Mother."

"The pig?"

"He tricked me." Agnes is babbling now, her hands ghosting around her ears like she's hearing voices. "I thought the bargain was good. But it wasn't. Mother had the blood, and he said all blood but ours must serve."

My mouth falls open more and more as Agnes tells me who and what Mother the pig was and is. There's hope for the others, then. There are ways out from under the mountain if you have luck and courage and wit.

But something she said catches up with me, and I ask, "You made the bargain we agreed on. Word for word. Didn't you?"

"He must leave us be. Him and the others. We have to fix this place so they can cross. But all other blood must serve, and he took Mother."

My guts turn to stone. Agnes is standing there all but crying, mourning a loss she can barely whisper and cursing herself for being dim enough to get tricked, so I choose my words carefully. "The bargain was that you and I would be able to live here free and untroubled. We forgot to say for how long, didn't we?"

Agnes's eyes widen. "Oh saints. We did."

I swear aloud. We are back on borrowed time, she and I, and once more bound by a bargain we cannot escape. The king will let us live untroubled, all right—until we've fulfilled our part of the bargain. All we've done is push back the inevitable.

Yet Agnes lifts her chin. I have never seen her angry, but now she looks like she could tear apart a fairy hill with her bare hands.

"Trick me, will he?" Agnes runs her fingers over the pit wall. "Well, I promised we'd fix the crossing place so Those Good People could ride. I never said how fast we'd do it."

She grins at me, huge and open. More than a little fierce. She's still saying *we*.

We drove handfuls of iron needles into the pit walls. Not a single one will be found easily. Our whole lives we'll be at it—a day here, an afternoon there—and yet we'll stay well within the terms of our bargain.

If they cannot ride, we will be safe.

I breathe out long and shaky. For a moment I was ready to give up. It's what you do, deep underground. Fairy trickery and cruelty will always win, so there's no point in fighting. But Agnes had no patience for such things. When the plan fell apart, she didn't follow it into pieces. Instead she changed the plan.

Mayhap there is something to this we.

Agnes tosses the shovel up onto the bank, then starts to climb. The scrap of fairy cloth is still in my hand, but the pattern is gone. There are no more greens woven into greens, ten thousand shades with the smallest bit of shimmer. It's simply green. A plain weave. Like any scrap of tattery cloth.

The boy-thing is dead.

I say as much to Agnes, but she shakes her head. "Those Good People cannot die."

I didn't think so either, but there's no other reason the fairy cloth would go dark like it has. It belonged to him, and he couldn't go home.

Agnes gets dressed and rebraids her hair, then we cross the heath toward the village. The air smells of green growing things, grass and wheat and countless kinds of flowers.

There's not even the faintest whiff of glamour. Trampled garlands lie everywhere, and strips of ground have been torn up by dancing feet. What's left of last night's revel. Sometimes I cannot help but wonder at the things that are the same. We danced and lit fires and made merry on this night, Acatica and me and our friends. Our parents, too, even though we teased them something awful, that old people should kiss behind the bushes so we would not have to watch. Our revel had a different name, but it's comforting to know something of it—something of us—survived the might of Rome.

Ma steps onto the threshold of the house, blinking in bewilderment. Then she sees us and throws her arms wide. All that glamour, and somehow Ma still knows she missed a year of Agnes. Agnes plows toward her, but I'm frozen. The fairy cloth is just cloth now, and there's no way I can know Ma will love me.

Agnes stops. Turns enough to see me standing alone. Then my friend backtracks, grabs my wrist, and tows me toward our ma, who is now rushing at us, pulling us both into a mighty two-arm hug.

I sink into her. Into my ma. I crack foreheads with Agnes, and we laugh.

"My girls," Ma is whispering, hoarse and throaty. "My girls."

One day I will tell her my real name. The one my first parents gave me and the one I would have my new parents embrace. I thought to take Agnes's place and become her so they would love me, but it's enough to be Senna. There is love enough here for that.

Agnes starts to pull away and Ma starts to let her, but I hold on. I have waited a thousand-thousand years for this. I am not letting go so easily.

Near the door, there's a small shrouded body wrapped up tidy and tight. There's no question about it. It's the boy-thing and he's dead. Ma and Da step around him as if he's a sack of barley. There is no mourning in this house. It's like the corpse is an empty bucket waiting to be stored in the shed.

Even now the fair folk will be keeping well away from the crossing place, their horses squealing and their swords sharp and reckless, and they are cursing us. They are free to curse. They're free to rail and tantrum and rage. Our blood doesn't matter. Not if they can't get to us. They are bound by a bargain, and those fairy wretches cannot go back on a bargain.

The boy-thing took my brother's face for his own ends, but there's something comforting about looking on it now. If I look past the green of this boy-thing, I will be able to finally say a proper farewell to my brother who died far from me and unburied.

Agnes appears at my side. "Do you think we did this?"

It's the only thing that makes sense. The Otherworld could not shield him from what we did to the crossing place. Or mayhap the walls stopped his heart by mistake as they lashed out in their ironsick delirium.

"I wanted him to go home and get better," she goes on quietly. "I didn't mean for him to die."

"Are you sorry?"

She pauses to consider, and I realize I like that about her. She doesn't just say the first thing that pops into her head. "Yes. It's always sad when something dies. Even something that means you harm. But the pit is there for a reason. We cannot have wolves in the village."

Ma is in the garden when Glory turns up at the door. Her eyes are still that fairy green, deep and swimming with tears.

"People are saying Martin is dead," she whispers. "But that cannot be true."

"He's gone," I tell her, and then I remember whose child she is and add, "The lord of this place thought to make Martin live at the manor house, but he didn't want to. So he went to the green land beyond the river. Where he came from."

Agnes starts to correct me, but I nudge her elbow and she snaps her mouth shut.

Glory's eyes widen. "You're not going too, are you?"

I shake my head. "I'm home, remember? The lord of

this place said I should live here. No better people to be my new ma and da. He said that. Remember?"

Glory nods slowly, even though she doesn't remember. She was nowhere near the manor house all those months ago when the reeve said as much.

"You'll tell your da, right?" I go on. "Sir Richard cannot take a girl away from her parents. I'll visit the manor house and talk to whoever he wants. I'll tell them about the river and the green land. Only I want to live here. All right?"

"I'll tell my da. I don't want you to go, too." Glory pets my sleeve like it's a kitten, then says faintly, "Martin's land. Only how will I look after him if he's there and I'm in Glory's land?"

"You can look after yourself instead," I reply gently. "Believe me, he never needed watching. You can sew with Kate and Tabby. You and Agnes and me can make flower crowns."

"Can't. Can't." Glory drifts off, worrying the tattery end of a cloak that should be retired to the rag bin. "Must find him."

Agnes looks anxious. "What's wrong with her? Ma and Da are back to normal. You said things would be as they were."

"What do you care?" I ask. "Do you have any idea the kinds of things she says about you?"

That makes Agnes pause, and bitter ghosts chase

themselves across her face one by one. At length she says, "I care for me. Because it feels better to care than to be hard inside. Even if I'm not her friend, she's still my friend."

"If you really want to help her, you'll let her believe he's gone," I reply.

Agnes is quiet for a long moment. "I can do that. There should be more stories where girls help one another."

Woolpit buries Martin in the churchyard on a bright May morning. A boy who arrived a stranger and became a son. A boy mourned by his foster parents, his sisters, his neighbors. So say the Woolpit mas, one to the other, until the village nods and knows it to be true.

"He was always sickly," Father says as we're leaving the funeral mass. "Some children are not long for this world."

The Woolpit das push back hoods and bow their heads. The mas murmur kindnesses to my parents, and they all speak fondly of the curiosity of a green boy in their midst. How he came from a verdant land beyond a broad, rushing river. How he was following his father's cattle and heard the bells of Saint Edmund's, then found himself with his sister in the wolf pit.

Senna takes me on her rounds. We help this ma with her milking and that ma with her garden. We bring dinners to the men and boys as they move down rows of greening wheat, pulling weeds and breaking clods. Chore by chore, errand by errand. The Woolpit mas smile and call me Agnes. They call her Agnes, too, but that's all right. We are both Agnes now.

There are a thousand stories in this place. If you have time, put your ear to the ground and close your eyes and wait. Every flower, every rock, is waiting to whisper in your ear. Woolpit would have you believe something simple and safe—there were green children and the harvesters found them. And it's true, in its own small way, but they're only repeating what they've heard. Far better to ask the girl in the story. The real tale is one only she can tell.

Ready?

It goes like this.

HISTORICAL NOTE

In the Middle Ages, two monks in different parts of England recorded a very similar and, to modern eyes, unlikely tale of two green-skinned children found near a village called Woolpit. Each monk told the story his own way, but they agreed on the core aspects of the event: The girl and boy were lost, they spoke a language no one understood, and they initially refused all food except raw beans. The boy grew sick and died, but the girl eventually learned to speak and described the place she'd come from—a green land where the sun never shone.

Medieval chronicles were kept for a number of reasons. We imagine them as careful, scrupulous records of important historical events, but this is not necessarily what the monks intended. They also wanted to make sense of the world as they understood it. It was common to include stories like the green children alongside happenings that we would view as "factual." When Ralph of Coggeshall and William of Newburgh recorded the story of the green children, they did so believing absolutely in the truth of the things they wrote, even if they didn't have an explanation.

Over the years, antiquarians, academics, folklorists, and writers have investigated, interpreted, and discussed the green children of Woolpit. Modern scholars have presented a number of rational explanations for the more outlandish aspects of the story in an attempt to separate fact from fiction. Many of these theories are convincing, but there are still things that don't add up. The folklorists, of course, point out how many elements of this story align with traditional fairy beliefs—the color green, the twilit world, the strange language, the refusal of food. Speculative fiction writers, one as early as the seventeenth century, have suggested that the green children came from other planets or even other dimensions. It seems that everyone wants a specific answer. We are all curious to know what *really* happened.

More than eight hundred years later, it's impossible to determine which parts of the green children story are real, which are misunderstood, which are misrepresented, and which are outright inventions. Trying to pin down the exact "truth" of a story like this one obscures a very real fact: Regardless of *when* you are, there is something deeply relatable about finding yourself in a place where you clearly don't belong. We may do better to follow the example of the monks themselves, who saw stories like this one as less a mystery to solve than a wonder to appreciate, enjoy, and share.

ACKNOWLEDGMENTS

My deepest thanks to:

Katherine Longshore, for keeping me honest and cheering me on.

Anne Nesbet, Nancy Day, Elizabeth Bunce, Jeanne Ryan, and Janet Lee Carey, for helping to unstick the sticky places.

Reka Simonsen, for her graceful, insightful, and indispensable guidance.

Ammi-Joan Paquette, for her tireless work on my behalf.

Julia McCarthy, for bringing a fresh perspective.

Victo Ngai, for the gorgeous, evocative cover art.

The team at Atheneum, for making this book lovely inside and out.

Readers everywhere, and the whole kid-lit community.